Redrum

Redrum

Boston George

www.urbanbooks.net

Urban Books, LLC
78 East Industry Court
Deer Park, NY 11729

ISBN 13: 978-1-60162-480-2
ISBN 10: 1-60162-480-8

First Printing December 2011
Printed in the United States of America

10 9 8 7 6 5 4 3 2 1

Distributed by Kensington Publishing Corp.
Submit Wholesale Orders to:
Kensington Publishing Corp.
C/O Penguin Group (USA) Inc.
Attention: Order Processing
405 Murray Hill Parkway
East Rutherford, NJ 07073-2316
Phone: 1-800-526-0275
Fax: 1-800-227-9604

Prologue

"Please, whatever I did, I swear I'm sorry," the light-skinned woman cried, looking around, trying to see where she was. She tried to move her arms then realized she was tied to the chair she sat in. She tried to move her legs next, but they were tied together.

"Where the fuck am I?" she cried as she felt something wet running down her leg. She figured it was blood, since she could feel her vagina throbbing in pain. The woman had been tied down to a hard wooden chair, and the naked bulb above her head threw her features into stark relief.

"I want to go home, pleasssssse!" she screamed.

Seconds later she heard a door open above her head, followed by slow, heavy footsteps, which grew louder and louder.

"I see you finally woke up." A man wearing a blue mechanic jumpsuit smiled.

"Perry, is that you?" The woman squinted her eyes to get a better look. "Perry, what the fuck are you doing, and where the fuck am I?"

"You're in my basement," he said calmly.

"Well, untie me," the woman said in a nasty tone.

"No can do," Perry said, shaking his head. "I'm about to give you just what you need." He smiled as he quickly disappeared back up the steps where he came from.

"Your ass is going straight to jail when I get out of here!" she yelled at his departing back. "You pervert muthafucka!"

Three minutes later Perry returned with two oven mitts on his hands, carrying a big pot of boiling water.

"Perry, what are you doing?" the woman asked, trying to hide the fear in her voice. "Whatever you thinking, please don't do it," she begged.

"I hate women like you." Perry looked at the woman in disgust. "You think because you're so pretty that you can just treat people however you feel like it."

"Perry, I'm sorry. Please give me another chance, and I swear I will never act like that again."

"People like you are too stuck in your ways." Perry sat the pot down on the floor. "You've been treating people like this for far too long to just be able to just stop like that. And now it's time to teach you a lesson." He pushed the woman's chair back so it was standing on its hind legs. He then slowly scooted the pot under the woman's feet with his leg.

"Perry, please don't do this. Please," the woman cried, hoping he would show her mercy.

But it was no use. Perry let the chair slam down, dropping the woman's feet directly inside the boiling pot.

"Ughhhhhhhhhhhhhhhh!" The woman screamed at the top of her lungs as she watched her feet boil in the pot.

The sight of the woman in so much pain brought a smile to Perry's face.

"And I got something for that pretty face of yours as well." He smiled as he pulled a street razor from his pocket, the blade only an inch and a half long.

"Please?" The woman looked down at the sharp blade in Perry's hand. "I didn't do nothing to deserve this," she cried out in pain.

Perry slowly walked up to the woman and stopped directly in front of her. "I'm doing the world a favor, trust me," he said as he firmly grabbed the woman's chin. He raised the blade and came down, cutting the woman's face with force.

Then he cut her again, and again, and again, and again, until the woman's face was a mask of horror. Blood dripped all over the basement floor as Perry stood there admiring his work. The woman was so badly hurt, she couldn't even scream any more. All she could do was let out soft moans like a wounded animal.

"Say good night," Perry whispered. He roughly jerked the woman's head back by her hair, and smoothly slit her throat with the blade.

The woman gargled on her blood as she tried to breathe. Her blood spilled out of her neck at a rapid pace. Then finally her neck hung tilted to the side, signaling she was dead.

"Hopefully, you've learned your lesson."

Perry smiled as he untied the woman and watched her body drop out the chair and slam against the floor. He grabbed her by her ankles and dragged her to the sleeping bag he had over in the corner. He dumped her body inside the sleeping bag and lifted the sleeping bag over his shoulder and carried it to his inside garage and dumped it in his trunk, which he slammed shut.

Diamond walked through her four-bedroom house wearing nothing but a yellow thong to match the color on her toes and finger nails, something she always did. Diamond, light-skinned with a nice shape, favored the actress Stacey Dash.

She stopped at the kitchen and poured herself a glass of red wine. As she sipped on her wine, she looked up at the big picture of her and Kendu on the wall. "He think he slick," she said to herself as she walked over

and grabbed the cordless phone from off the charger.
Kendu was supposed to have been home hours ago.
She dialed his number and waited patiently as his
phone rang.

"How much is this?" Kendu asked, looking at the
money that was tightly wrapped in a rubber band.

"Four thousand," his right-hand man Deuce replied,
gun in hand.

"Nah. I know this clown got more money up in
this house somewhere," Kendu said, looking around
the apartment, tearing it up as he went along. Kendu
walked over to the man and wife he had tied up laying face down on the floor. He viciously snatched the
duct tape from the man's mouth. "Where's the rest of
the money?" he asked. "I know you got more than four
thousand up in here."

"Fuck you!" the man spat, mad that he had been
caught slipping. "You lucky you even got that!"

Kendu smiled as he pulled his .45 from the small of
his back. "Did you just say fuck me?" He pressed the
gun to the back of the man's head.

Immediately the man's wife started going crazy. She
was trying to say something, but since her mouth was
taped, all that came out was loud muffles.

"You got something you want to tell me?" Kendu
asked, looking over at the wife.

She nodded her head up and down.

"If you ain't telling me where the money is, I'm going to allow you to watch me kill your husband. You
understand?" Kendu snatched the tape from the wife's
mouth, taking off the little bit of hair she had on her
upper lip. "You better make it good," he said, his .45
now aimed at her head.

"Fuck him, baby!" the husband yelled. "Don't tell him shit!"

The wife ignored her husband's words. "The rest of the money is in the basement," she said. "Look in the washing machine, and you'll find a duffel bag inside."

"Go check it out." Kendu watched Deuce disappear down into the basement.

"Now, was that so hard?" He chuckled when he saw Deuce return from the basement carrying a duffel bag.

"She just saved your life," Kendu said to the husband as he and Deuce exited the house.

Outside Deuce hopped in the driver's seat of the getaway car. Once Kendu slid in the passenger seat, Deuce put the pedal to the metal.

"That's what I'm talking about," Deuce said excitedly as he drove normally.

"I told you that was going to be an easy lick." Kendu felt his iPhone vibrating on his hip. He looked at the caller ID and saw that it was Diamond. "Hello," he answered.

"Don't hello me," Diamond said with heavy attitude. "I been calling you all day. Where you been?"

"I was out taking care of a little business," Kendu explained.

"Well, when are you coming home so you can take care of this business?" She rubbed on her breast as if he could see her through the phone.

"I'm going to split up this money with Deuce then I'm coming straight home," he told her.

"A'ight. Be careful, baby," Diamond said as she ended the call.

Two hours later Diamond sat in the living room watching the news when she saw Kendu walk through the front door. "Hey, baby," she sang as she slid in his arms and hugged him tightly.

"Hey, baby," Kendu said as he palmed both of her ass cheeks as he hugged her. "How was your day?"

"It was cool," she replied. "I was just watching the news"—she stopped to shake her head—"they found some schoolteacher's body all chopped up in an alley. They said her feet were burnt up pretty bad."

"It's some crazy-ass people out here," Kendu said as he headed upstairs so he could take a shower.

Kendu stepped out the shower with a towel wrapped around his waist. He stepped out of the bathroom and saw Diamond spread across the bed butt naked, wearing nothing but some heels. The only light in the room was from the four candles she had lit up.

Kendu felt his equipment begin to rise quickly. "Damn! You looking sexy."

"How sexy?" Diamond purred as she turned over on her back, opened her legs and began playing with her pussy. When she was finished, she stuck her fingers in her mouth and sucked away the juices. "I saved you some," she said in a seductive tone.

With that invitation Kendu let his towel drop to the floor as he headed over towards the bed. Immediately he stuck his face in her pussy and began licking and sucking all over her clit like he had just been released from a ten-year prison sentence.

"Yeah, daddy," Diamond moaned, gyrating her hips and wrapping her legs around his head as she released in his mouth.

After her orgasm Diamond turned over on all fours, anticipating the dick. Kendu eased up behind her and entered her nice and slow.

***

"Damn!" Kendu moaned as he felt Diamond's pussy grip his dick as he slid in and out of her at a nice pace. As he slapped her ass, he watched as Diamond's ass bounced off his torso with each stroke.

Just as Kendu was about to come, he quickly pulled out. Immediately Diamond spun around and started sucking the shit out of his dick, jerking it with one hand, and cupping his balls with the other, until he exploded in her mouth with a loud grunt.

Diamond swallowed before she spoke. "Who's the best?"

"You are, baby," he said out of breath as he lay across the bed, looking like he was dead.

"I love you, baby," Diamond said over her shoulder as she disappeared in the bathroom to take a quick shower.

Twenty minutes later Diamond stepped out the bathroom and saw Kendu knocked out cold. Immediately her eyes went over to his cell phone that rested on the dresser. At first she dismissed the thought from her mind, but then something inside of her just wanted to know. She walked over to the dresser and picked up her husband's iPhone. She opened it and went straight to his incoming and outgoing calls.

She saw calls from herself, Deuce, and another woman named Carmen. "Who the fuck is this bitch?" Diamond wondered out loud. She tapped the girl's name on the phone, and immediately the phone dialed her number.

Diamond stepped out the room and headed downstairs to the living room to avoid waking Kendu and getting caught. The phone rang six times before a woman answered.

"Hey, baby," she said happily.

"Hey, baby, *my ass!*" Diamond barked. "What the fuck is you doing calling my husband so many times in a day? And who the fuck is you calling *baby*?"

"First of all, who is this?" Carmen looked at the phone like whoever was on the other line was crazy.

"This is Kendu's wife," Diamond said with authority. "And I want to know why the fuck is your number all throughout my husband's phone?"

"Me and Kendu are just friends," Carmen countered, shaking her head at the jealous woman on the other end of the phone.

"So you call all of your friends *baby*?"

"Look, I just told you me and Kendu are just friends." Carmen lied 'cause she knew if she disrespected Kendu's wife, he would never speak to her again.

"Whatever, bitch!" Diamond growled. "I'ma fuck you up when I catch your triflin' ass," she yelled as she ended the call. She headed back upstairs and angrily snatched the covers off Kendu's naked body.

"Fuck is you doing?" Kendu asked, squinting his eyes, not knowing what was going on.

"Who the fuck is Carmen?" she asked, her arms folded across her chest.

Kendu tried to stall for time, so he could think. "Who?"

"Don't play stupid with me," she snapped. "You know exactly who I'm talking about."

"She's just a girl whose house I stash money at from time to time."

"You must think I'm a damn fool," Diamond said as she slid in the bed. "It's okay, though. 'Cause when I go and give somebody some of this good-ass pussy, we going to see how much you like it."

"If you ever give my shit away, I'll break your face. You are my wife." He paused. "But yet you out here worrying about these other women that mean nothing to me."

"They must mean something, 'cause you out here fuckin' them."

"I ain't fuckin' nobody," Kendu said, and the conversation was left at that.

For the rest of the night the two of them slept with their backs towards one another, not saying a word until they drifted off to sleep.

Chapter 1

Kendu pulled up at the gas station that him and Deuce always met up at. "What's good, five?" he said as him and Deuce slapped hands.

"Same shit, different tissue," Deuce replied, his eyes alert to the passing cars. "What's the plan for today?" he asked.

"That new trap house we set up been bringing in some all right numbers," Kendu said. "Let's slide through there and pick up that re-up money." He slid in his work vehicle, a '99 Acura, nothing too flashy. Cops harassing him was the last thing Kendu needed. "Keep up," he yelled out the window as he pulled off.

Deuce quickly followed Kendu's lead, pulling off right behind the Acura in his Chevy Malibu.

Kendu pulled up a block away from the trap house and let the engine die. Seconds later he saw Deuce in his rearview mirror pull up behind him.

The two men walked around to the back door. Outside the back door stood a line of about five fiends waiting.

Seconds later a young teenaged kid came out the back door and served each fiend on the line, quickly getting rid of them. The teenager looked up and smiled. "What up, Kendu?" he said with his hand extended.

Kendu looked at the young teenager like he was retarded, walking right past him, and bumping him in the process. He walked in the trap house and stopped as soon as he reached the kitchen. Immediately he saw three empty boxes of baking soda on the counter, and a sink full of dishes with plenty of evidence on them. "Yo', where the fuck is Spider?"

Deuce smirked as he went upstairs in search of Spider. When he made it upstairs, he noticed that all the room doors were open, except for one. Immediately he walked over to the door and placed his ear to the door. On the other side of the door he heard what sounded like moaning coming from behind the door. Deuce quickly took a step back, came forward, and kicked open the door. Inside Spider sat in a chair with a hood rat-looking chick on her knees in between his legs.

"Yo', Deuce, what's good?" Spider asked, giving him the "can't-you-see-I'm-busy" look.

"Nigga, Kendu downstairs." Deuce smirked. "He wants to see you."

"Damn! 'Cause Kendu downstairs, you had to kick the door open?" Spider joked. "Niggas don't knock no more nowadays." He quickly pulled up his pants and followed Deuce downstairs.

By the look on Kendu's face, Spider could tell he was in trouble for something. "What's good, my *G*?" Spider said, his hand out for some dap.

"You want to go to jail?" Kendu said, ignoring Spider's extended hand. "If the cops kick in this door, they ain't gon' need to find nothing, 'cause all the evidence is right there in the sink."

"Nah, I was just about to clean that shit up," Spider said, putting his hand down. "But—"

"What's taking so long, Spider?" The hood rat came downstairs popping her gum extra loud for no reason. She looked at him for some answers.

"Yo', don't you hear me talking?" Spider said coldly, knowing she just got him in even more trouble than he was already in. "Matter of fact, bitch, get your shit and get the fuck out of here!" he yelled as he forcefully shoved her out the door.

Kendu just shook his head in disgust. "I chose you to run our trap house, and this is what you do with the opportunity?"

"Nah, it's not even like that," Spider said. "I mean, at least I got the money straight."

"You don't get no points for that," Deuce cut in. "I told you, you shouldn't of put this nigga in charge," he said, looking at Kendu.

"Nah, just give me another chance. You got my word. I won't let you down." Spider didn't want to mess up his only source of income.

Kendu pointed in Spider's direction. "This is a fuckin' business, not no fuckin' whorehouse. Smell me? Keep ya fuckin' nasty-ass bitches the fuck up out of here." He shook his head. "Got bitches in here and the kitchen still dirty."

"My word, something like this will never happen again," Spider tried to assure him.

"It better not—unless you wanna be a muthafuckin' lookout."

Deuce laughed out loud.

"Now where that paper at?"

Kendu and Deuce watched as Spider trooped up the steps.

Minutes later he returned carrying a JanSport book bag. "Here," he said, handing Kendu the bag. "It's straight."

"It better be." Kendu handed the book bag over to Deuce. He was about to say something else, until he heard some loud banging on the back door. He watched as the young teenager slowly bopped to the door and yelled at the fiend before serving him.

"Yo', my man." Kendu waved the teenager over.

"What up?" the teenager said with a smile on his face.

Kendu quickly removed the smile from the kid's face when he dug down in his pocket and took all the money he had on him. "Now get the fuck outta here!" he barked.

"Bu—but what did I do?" the teenager asked, a confused look on his face.

"Fam, I said get the fuck outta here!" Kendu repeated in a sterner tone.

The teenager asked with a mean look on his face, "Can I at least get my jacket from upstairs?"

"Nigga!" Deuce growled as he stole on the teen, dropping him with a quick right hook. "Talk too fuckin' much! The man said get the fuck out!"

"Listen. Find me somebody else to serve the fiends. Somebody who wants to work. This ain't no movie," Kendu said seriously. "And I want the fiends coming to the front door. Let them in, serve them, then send them on they way out the back door. In and out like a robbery. I don't want to see no fuckin' lines and shit outside," he said, looking to see if Spider was paying attention. "Start treating this shit like a business, and not a hustle."

"You right," Spider said, knowing he was wrong.

"And clean this shit up," Kendu said, looking at the kitchen, him and Deuce getting ready to leave.

"Hold up," Spider said, stopping them before they left. "Word on the streets is one of Dirty Black's boys got robbed the other day."

"Yeah, and?" Kendu shrugged his shoulders.

"And the streets is saying it was you who robbed him," Spider informed him.

"And what they saying about Dirty Black?" Kendu asked curiously.

"Nothing yet," Spider answered. "But you know it won't be long until he finds out."

"Fuck Dirty Black!" Kendu spat. "I ain't hard to find," he said as him and Deuce exited the trap house.

Kendu and Deuce sat in IHOP getting their eat on, waiting on somebody who wanted to buy ten pounds of weed. "I got this plan on how we can up on some real paper." Deuce cut his pancakes and stuffed a forkful in his mouth.

"How?"

"I say we should open up a whorehouse," Deuce suggested.

Kendu laughed, almost spilling his orange juice. "A whorehouse?" he repeated.

"I don't see why not," Deuce said seriously. "I mean, pussy never stops selling."

"Nah, I ain't no pimp," Kendu said, turning down his idea. "I do what I know. I don't got no time for some dumb shit to be happening right now. We almost right where we need to be," he reminded his partner.

"You right," Deuce agreed, but deep down he liked his idea and really felt that it could work. He hated how Kendu always shot down his ideas without even giving them any thought. "Ain't that that clown right there?" Deuce motioned his head towards the two men coming their way.

Mousey walked up with his main goon close on his heels, and the two men helped themselves to a seat. "Gentlemen," Mousey said as he gave Kendu and Deuce a pound.

"Took you long enough to get here," Kendu huffed, mad that Mousey had him waiting.

"My bad," Mousey apologized. "Traffic was crazy," he said, placing the book bag he held in his hands under the table in between Kendu's legs. In return Deuce handed Mousey the bag with the weed under the table.

"Nice doing business with you." Kendu head-signaled for Mousey to leave.

"I want to talk a little business with you before I bounce," Mousey said, a grimy look in his eyes.

"What's on your mind?" Kendu's eyes never left his plate as he cut up his pancakes.

"I was thinking that maybe my team and your team should team up and take shit over," Mousey said. "Us together would be unstoppable."

"What's the benefits both ways?" Kendu asked. "'Cause we good over here."

"I mean," Mousey began, "you got the connect, and I got the soldiers. We getting money, but we could be getting more money if we had your connect."

Kendu finally looked up. "And what would I get out of this deal?"

"I'm bringing muscle to the table," Mousey said with a smirk on his face. "I mean, I heard about the shit with you and Dirty Black, and you know I roll with nothing but gorillas, so you'll be straight."

"I'm already straight," Kendu said, not liking how Mousey's last statement came out.

"Not like that," Mousey said, trying to clean up his last statement. "All I'm trying to say is us together would be un-*fuckin'*-stoppable."

"Thanks, but no thanks." Kendu wiped his mouth with a napkin. "We good how we are right now. And if it ain't broke, I ain't going to try to fix it."

"But think about all the money we could make."

"Listen, fam," Kendu said, "I fuck with what I know, and I know I've made it in this game a long time sticking to what I know, and that's how I'ma keep it."

"A'ight, cool." Mousey stood up to leave. "If y'all change y'all's mind, holla at me," he said as him and his boy exited the restaurant.

Once the two men left the restaurant, Deuce spoke up. "That sounded like a good deal he proposed to us."

"Fuck him!" Kendu said coldly. "A nigga like that can't be trusted. He's too greedy."

"But what he was saying was right. If he got all the goons, then we won't have to worry about Dirty Black's peoples coming at us from all angles."

"You sound like you scared." Kendu chuckled. "Let me find out this nigga Dirty Black got you shook."

"Please," Deuce said. "I ain't scared of nobody. I just know what the nigga is capable of."

"Anybody can pull a trigger," Kendu said as he got up. He paid the bill then left. He pretended that the Dirty Black situation didn't bother him, but the truth was, it was at the front of his mind.

After Kendu and Deuce finished splitting up the money, Kendu shot over to Carmen's house. He did the special knock that he always did, and seconds later Carmen opened the door with a smile on her face.

"What took you so long to get here?"

"My bad. I had to take care of a few things," Kendu said, stepping inside the crib.

He looked at Carmen and noticed that she wore a red camisole with the matching thong, her hair thrown back in an effortless ponytail. Carmen favored the singer Toni Braxton. She was definitely a lady in the streets, and a super freak behind closed doors.

"You like my outfit?" Carmen asked, flashing a pose so Kendu could get a good look at her ass.

"I love it." Kendu thought Carmen looked real sexy in her outfit. "Why you got all this sexy shit on? You know I can't stay long," he reminded her as he handed her a book bag full of cash.

"I know we pushed for time, but I thought I'd make the best out of the little time we do have." Carmen seductively applied lip gloss after stacking Kendu's money in his safe.

"What did you have in mind?" Kendu asked with a smirk on his face.

"Glad you asked." Carmen pushed Kendu down on the couch as she squatted down in between his legs and removed his pants. "I see somebody missed me," she said, referring to Kendu's manhood sitting at attention. She slowly wrapped her soft lips around his pipe as she tickled the head with her tongue. "You like that?" she asked in a seductive voice. She stroked Kendu's dick while looking in his eyes. "You want some more?"

Kendu didn't reply. Instead, he just pushed Carmen's head back down as he watched her make his dick disappear in and out of her mouth at a fast pace. "Damn," he whispered as he stood up and began fucking Carmen's mouth like it was a pussy. Carmen took each stroke like a pro as she continued to suck the shit out of Kendu's dick, until he exploded all in her mouth.

"Damn! That was quick," Carmen said as she stood up. "Wifey must not be handling her duties at home?"

"Shit been fucked up at home ever since she spoke to you on the phone the other night."

"Sorry about that, baby. I swear I didn't tell her nothing."

"I know you didn't, baby." Kendu gave Carmen a hug. "I'ma call you later, a'ight?"

"Okay, baby." Carmen watched the man she loved make his exit.

"When you coming home?" Diamond asked.

"I'm on my way right now," Kendu replied. "I should be there in about twenty minutes."

"Okay, I'm going to run to the liquor store and grab us some wine real quick," Diamond said.

"A'ight, and grab me some Grey Goose."

Diamond quickly threw on some black jeans, a black shirt, and slipped her feet inside her Ugg boots. She threw her hair in a ponytail, put on a thin jacket, and headed out the door. She hopped in her new Infiniti G35 and flew out the driveway like a bat out of hell.

Diamond pulled up in the liquor store parking lot and was pissed when a new Lexus coupe pulled into the last parking spot. "Muthafucka!" she yelled as she beeped her horn at the Lexus.

"Damn," she mumbled when she saw the tall dark-skinned man step out the Lexus and make his way towards her car. "Damn, he fine," she said to herself as she saw the man approaching. The Derek Luke look-alike slowly walked up to Diamond's window and tapped on it.

"Yes," Diamond said with an attitude as she slightly cracked the window.

"Did you want that spot?" he asked.

"I know you saw me headed for that spot," she said, rolling her eyes.

"Sorry. I thought you was a guy," he told her. "I didn't know you was so beautiful. Hi, my name is Perry," he said, holding out his hand.

Diamond rolled down her window and shook his hand. "I'm Diamond."

"The name fits you perfectly," Perry said, openly flirting.

Diamond saw an open spot right next to Perry's Lexus. "Let me get that spot before somebody takes it," she said and quickly pulled into the spot.

She stepped out her car and headed inside the liquor store, with Perry close on her heels.

"So," Perry began, "you live around here?" he asked as he picked up an expensive bottle of champagne.

Diamond turned around to face the handsome man. "Listen, you seem like a real cool person and all, but I'm married. Sorry."

"Does that mean we can't be friends?" Perry asked with his million-dollar smile.

"That's exactly what it means," Diamond said as she walked over and grabbed her two bottles of wine, and one bottle of Grey Goose. "It was nice meeting you, though." She placed her bottles up on the counter and paid for them.

"See you around." Perry watched her walk from the store all the way back to her car.

Diamond watched Perry watch her as she pulled out of the parking spot and headed home.

Diamond pulled up in her driveway and saw Kendu's car sitting there. *About time he brought his black ass home*, she thought, as she slid out her whip and headed inside the house.

"Hey, baby. What's up?" Kendu said, sitting at the kitchen table, counting money. "You got my Goose?"

"Right here," Diamond replied, holding up the bag. "You missed me while you was out running the streets?" She kissed her husband on the lips.

"I always miss you, baby," Kendu said, never taking his eyes off the money. "I just be having a lot of shit on my mind, you dig?"

"Well, maybe if you talk to your wife, I might can help you," Diamond said as she slid in his lap.

"I think I done fucked around and robbed the wrong nigga this time, baby," Kendu told her.

"What happened?" Diamond knew it had to be bad if Kendu was concerned.

"Robbed some nigga named Dirty Black." Kendu paused. "The nigga is large out here in the streets."

"Yeah, I think of heard of him," Diamond said. "So what you going to do if he try to get at you?"

"You already know," Kendu said, tapping the ratchet on his waistline.

"Please be careful out there in them streets."

"I got everything under control, baby," Kendu said in an unbelievable voice.

"Come upstairs so I can give you a massage." Diamond grabbed Kendu's hand and led him upstairs to the bedroom. She could tell that her husband had a lot on his mind, and figured a nice hot oil massage should make him feel a little better.

Chapter 2

Perry looked up at himself in the mirror as he washed fresh blood from his hands. Just thinking about what he had just done brought an evil smirk to his face. He reached over and grabbed a washrag and placed it under the faucet. After he slowly rung out the rag, he wiped the blood specks off his handsome face. He turned to his right and saw the blond-haired woman laid in a tub full of ammonia, with over a hundred cuts and slices on her body. The duct tape over her mouth prevented her from screaming.

"How you feeling?" Perry asked with a smirk on his face as he snatched the tape from the woman's mouth.

"Please, I'm begging you," the woman began. "Please let me go."

"Sorry, no can do," Perry said, shaking his head. "You should of thought about that before you failed my test."

"What test?" the woman asked in a weak voice. "You can't go around killing people because you don't like something about them." The woman sobbed.

"Women who think they too good for the rest of the world because of how beautiful they are shouldn't be allowed to walk this earth. All I'm doing is cleaning up this fucked up world." Perry believed every word he spoke. He had given the woman his test, and she had failed it miserably. Now she had to pay.

"You are a fucked up individual, and I hope you get what you deserve." the white woman spat in Perry's face. "Do what you gotta do," she said, closing her eyes, anticipating the pain she knew was on the way.

Perry pulled out his street razor and firmly grabbed the woman's chin. He threw his arm in the air and came down with force, and the blade left a nasty cut on her face. Perry repeated that motion over and over again until the white woman's face looked like a cross-word puzzle. "Dirty-ass bitch!" Perry hawked and spat in the woman's face. He walked over and grabbed the plugged-in lamp from off the little table that sat over in the corner.

"Fuck you, Perry!" The woman began praying out loud.

Perry stopped about three or four feet from the tub and tossed the lamp inside the tub with the woman still inside. He watched as her body jerked and jumped like a fish fresh out of water. Once the woman's body stopped jerking, Perry just shook his head at the smoking bathtub.

Carmen stood in front of her full body mirror applying lotion on her sexy smooth legs. The only thing on her mind was Kendu. Even though she knew he was married, she was still in love with him. And she didn't mind being his number two. The way she saw it, it was better to have a piece of him than none at all. As she stood in front of the mirror, she paused when she thought she heard a noise. Seconds later she heard a loud *BOOM!* followed by glass shattering.

"Oh my God!" Carmen screamed. She ran over towards her cordless phone as she heard loud footsteps running throughout her house. She reached the phone and desperately tried to dial Kendu's number, but a strong punch to her face stopped her in mid-dial.

Carmen screamed out in pain as she fell on the floor. She looked up and saw two masked men standing over her, one man holding a shotgun, the other a Desert Eagle.

"Bitch, get yo' ass up!" The shorter one of the two men grabbed a handful of Carmen's hair, helping her back up to her feet. "I'm only going to ask you this once," he growled. "Where's the money?"

"What money?" Carmen replied with a scared look on her face.

As soon as those words left her mouth, she immediately felt the Desert Eagle slap her across the face, dropping her on impact.

The gunman aimed his Desert Eagle at Carmen's head and pulled the trigger, aiming slightly to the right, missing her head by inches on purpose. "Last time. Where's the money? And I promise the next time I won't miss."

"It's over there in the safe," Carmen said, her head hung low.

"What's the combination?" the gunman asked in a menacing voice.

"Thirty-five, eighteen, six," she answered in a low voice, feeling like she had just let Kendu down.

Immediately the second gunman raced over to the safe and put in the combination. The door on the safe immediately popped open, and Carmen watched as the second gunman greedily filled up the black garbage bag.

"Y'all clowns must not know who y'all fuckin' with," Carmen huffed. "When my man finds out what happened, he going to have y'all heads in a bag!"

The shorter gunman smirked from behind his mask. He walked over and kicked Carmen dead in her face. "You got a lot of mouth, bitch!" he growled, getting on top of her and rearranging her face with his Desert Eagle.

After thirty seconds of pounding her face in with the gun, the second gunman had to come in and stop him. "That's enough, muthafucka!" he yelled, pulling the shorter gunman off Carmen's body. "We was supposed to take the money and leave. That's it!" He yelled as he grabbed his shotgun and ran out the house.

The shorter gunman stomped Carmen in her face one last time before he followed his partner and ran up out the house, leaving Carmen for dead.

Kendu laid in the bed with Diamond laying on his chest as they watched episodes of *Martin* on DVD.

"This nigga is hilarious." Diamond laughed.

Diamond was so excited to finally be able to spend some quality time with Kendu. If he wasn't out taking care of business, he was running the streets. But not tonight. Tonight she had him all to herself, and she was loving every second of it.

She rested her head on Kendu's chest as the two laughed their asses off.

"Oh hell no," she fussed when she heard Kendu's phone ring.

"Hello?" Kendu answered.

"Baby?" Carmen said weakly.

"Carmen, is that you?" Kendu asked.

"Baby, they took the money," Carmen said, barely able to get the words out. "I tried to stop them. I swear I did."

"I'm on my way," Kendu said, hanging up the phone.

Diamond hopped up. "I know you don't think you going over there to see that bitch," she huffed, folding her arms across her chest. "Tonight is supposed to be *Our* time," she said, dragging out the word.

"I have to go, baby. Some serious shit just happened," Kendu said as he got dressed in a hurry.

"Why the fuck you always have to go? Why can't Deuce go take care of that?"

Kendu ignored her as he grabbed his .45 and headed downstairs for the front door. Diamond quickly ran past him and stood in front of the door, to prevent him from leaving. "No! Fuck that!"

"Come on, baby. Don't start this shit tonight."

"Nope," Diamond said. "This is our night tonight, and you ain't leaving me to go be with the next bitch."

Kendu took a deep breath. Then he scooped Diamond up by her legs, removed her from in front of the door as she beat on his back and the top of his head like a drum, then exited the house.

"Fuck you!" Diamond yelled from the doorway. "Go be with that bitch! I don't give a fuck!" She slammed the door.

Diamond flopped down on the couch as tears escaped from her eyes. She hated that another woman could call and make her husband run out the door. "Fuck him!" she said as she wiped her eyes and headed back upstairs.

Kendu just shook his head as he pulled out of his driveway and headed straight for Carmen's house. During the ride over there, he thought the worst. From the sound of Carmen's voice, he knew somebody had hurt her real bad.

He pulled up in front of Carmen's house and saw her front door wide open. "Fuck!" He snatched his .45 from his waistband and hopped out his car. He slowly crept up to the front door, not sure if any intruders were still inside. He stepped inside the house with a two-handed grip on his gun and slowly eased his way through the house.

Kendu finally made his way upstairs and saw Carmen laid out on the floor, wearing nothing but a thong, in a puddle of her own blood. "Fuck!" He kneeled down by her side. Before he said another word, he looked over to his right and saw that the door to his safe was wide open. Immediately he knew what went down.

"I'm sorry, daddy," Carmen said through a pair of busted lips.

Kendu pulled out his iPhone and dialed 9-1-1.

"I tried to stop them," she said in a light whisper.

"How many of them was it?"

"Two."

"Did you see any of their faces?"

Carmen shook her head no.

"Everything going to be fine," Kendu told her as he looked at the caller ID on his phone and saw Diamond's name flashing across the screen. He immediately sent her straight to voice mail. Right now he didn't have time to be arguing with her, especially over some bullshit. "Try not to talk," Kendu said. "The ambulance will be here any second."

Diamond cursed loudly when she got Kendu's voice mail. She just knew he was over there fucking Carmen. Why else would he send her straight to voice mail? "Oh, he think it's a game," she thought out loud as she went upstairs and hopped in the shower. She was tired of sitting at home always crying. Tonight she was going to put her foot down.

An hour later Diamond stood in the mirror looking at her appearance. She wore a tight-fitting all-white tube dress, with some red three-inch heels that wrapped around her calves, to match her red headband. "This nigga must be stupid, if he think I'ma just be sitting around while he out with another bitch," Diamond said out loud to herself. She applied her M·A·C lip gloss on her full lips, grabbed her red Coach bag and keys from off the table, and headed out the door.

Kendu watched as the paramedics placed Carmen in the back of the ambulance. "If you hear anything, feel free to give me a call," a Chinese detective said as he handed Kendu his card.

"I got you," Kendu replied politely.

As soon as the detective walked off, Kendu tossed the card to the ground and spat on it. "What a mutha-fuckin' day!" he said out loud. He pinched the bridge of his nose, thinking of who could have been behind this.

He walked over to his car and pulled an old weed clip from out of his ashtray and placed it between his lips. Then he pulled out his cell phone and dialed Deuce's number.

"I told you that shit was going to be like taking candy from a baby," Deuce said as him Mousey sat at the table counting out how much money they just took from Carmen's crib.

"That nigga Kendu is a clown. I knew that shit was going to be easy," Mousey boasted.

"Fuck all that! You didn't have to do Carmen the way you did."

"What?" Mousey looked at Deuce like he was insane. "The bitch started popping off at the mouth. What was I supposed to do?"

"Scare her a little bit."

"Fuck a scare!" Mousey said. "Let's just figure out how we going to take Kendu out the game."

"What did you have in mind?"

"I say we just kill him. Fuck it!" Mousey said, rubbing his beard.

"I can't just kill him just like that," Deuce said. "We grew up together."

"Fuck all that! This shit is all about business," Mousey huffed. "And in this business it ain't no time for games. The only way we going to get to the top is to shoot our way up there," he said, trying to get Deuce to see things his way.

"I feel you." Deuce heard his cell phone ringing. He looked at his phone and saw Kendu's name flashing across the screen. "It's Kendu."

"Answer it," Mousey told him. "Act regular like everything is all good."

Deuce nodded his head. "Hello?"

"Yo', somebody just hit my stash at Carmen's crib!" Kendu said, fire in his tone.

"Get the fuck outta here! You bullshitting," Deuce said, playing the role.

"Word!" Kendu said. "I think that nigga Dirty Black had something to do with this."

"Where you at right now?"

"I'm still at Carmen's crib."

"A'ight. I'm on my way right now," Deuce said, ending the call. Deuce gave Mousey a pound. "I'ma holla at you later."

Chapter 3

Diamond walked to the club's entrance with a frown on her face. The line to get inside was around the corner. She quickly took a glance at each of the bouncers' faces to see if she knew one of them so she wouldn't have to wait on the long-ass line. "Fuck!" She headed to the back of the line, her heels clicking loudly on the pavement with each step.

Just as she reached the back of the line, she heard a familiar voice say, "I know you not about to wait on this long-ass line."

Diamond turned around, and in front of her stood the handsome man from the other night, and once again he was looking fine as ever. "Well, how else am I supposed to get in?" she said with a slight attitude.

"Follow me," Perry said as he headed toward the club's entrance.

Diamond followed close behind. When they reached the entrance, Perry leaned in and whispered something in one of the bouncers' ear. Then he turned to face Diamond. "Go inside, and I'm going to catch up with you later on."

"Thank you," Diamond said seductively as she walked inside the club.

Diamond stepped inside the club and saw that it was already packed inside. "Damn," she said, squeezing and bumping her way through the live crowd until she reached the bar, where she ordered her drink. She

then turned towards the crowd and watched other partygoers get their freak on. She took her drink from the
bartender then disappeared back into the crowd. She
found a seat on the couch over in the corner.

Before she could even sit down, a fight broke out.
The crowd in the middle of the dance floor formed a
circle as the two men went blow for blow until three big
bouncers came and broke up the fight.

"Damn!" Diamond huffed. She hated that whenever
too many black people got together the outcome was
always violence.

Once the fight was broken up, everyone continued to
get their party on like nothing ever happened.

She noticed Perry heading in her direction.

"Damn! I been looking all over for you," he said with
a smile. "Why you over here hiding in the cut?"

"I don't like being all up in the spotlight. That's not
even my flow." She took a sip of her drink.

"Well, I'm glad to know we have at least one thing in
common." Perry smiled. "What's that you drinking?"

"Wine," Diamond answered quickly.

"What kind?"

"Moscato."

Perry grabbed a bouncer that stood close to him and
whispered something in his ear.

"So do you like own this place or something?" Diamond noticed Perry seemed to be calling shots.

"Actually, I do," Perry told her.

Seconds later the bouncer returned with a bottle of
Moscato. "Good looking." Perry took the bottle from
him and handed it to Diamond.

"Thank you."

"It's nothing," Perry said, fanning her off.

Little did Diamond know, but Perry was paid, and
didn't mind spending money. He'd been rich for so
long that he spent money like it was nothing.

Seconds later the club went crazy when Lloyd Banks'
song, "Beamer, Benz, or Bentley," came blaring through
the speakers. Perry grabbed Diamond's hand and
pulled her up out of her seat. Immediately Diamond's
started gyrating her hips to the beat, the whole time
looking Perry in his eyes.

"Damn!" Perry mumbled when he saw how effortlessly Diamond's ass began to jiggle as she swayed her
hips.

Diamond got low and grinded her ass up against
Perry's penis as she put it on him. And Perry held his
own on the dance floor, until another fight broke out,
causing the DJ to stop the music.

"Come on, let's get up out of here and get us something to eat," Perry said as he grabbed Diamond's hand
and led her outside.

"Hold up." Diamond went back and grabbed her
bottle of Moscato then returned back by Perry's side.

"Let's get up out of here," he said as he led her towards the exit. Once outside Perry led Diamond to his
all-black 745 BMW.

"What about my car?" Diamond asked.

"After we eat, I'll swing back around here and drop
you off to your car." Perry opened up the passenger
door for her then slid behind the wheel.

Deuce pulled up in front of Carmen's house and saw
Kendu sitting on the steps with his head buried in his
hands. "Damn," he mumbled, feeling bad for his friend
and partner in crime. Inside he felt like a fucked up
person, but on the outside he knew he had to get paid
by any means necessary, especially since Kendu always
turned down all of his ideas. Deuce loved Kendu like a
brother, but he loved money more, and decided that he

would no longer be looked over, or have his ideas put on the back burner. It was now his time to shine.

He slipped out the driver's seat and walked over to the front of the house where Kendu sat. "My nigga, you a'ight?" Deuce asked, his voice full of concern.

"They damn near killed her," Kendu said, raising his head from his hands. "When I find out who was behind this shit, I'm going to leave his brains on the curb."

"Whatever you wanna do, you know I'm down to ride," Deuce told him. "You think that nigga Dirty Black had something to do with this?"

"I don't know, but you better believe I'm going to find out." Kendu had robbed plenty of people in his day, but now he was on the other side of the coin and didn't like it at all.

"You wanna run down on something tonight?" Deuce asked.

"Nah. I'm just gonna go home and think about what just happened." He gave Deuce a pound, slid in his Acura, and peeled off.

Kendu pulled up in front of his house, and immediately noticed that Diamond's car wasn't in the driveway. "Where the fuck she at?" He hopped out his car and entered his house. Kendu stepped in the crib and smelled Diamond's perfume throughout the house. He quickly pulled out his cell phone and dialed her number.

Diamond sat in the small restaurant checking Perry out on the low while she cut up her steak. Damn! *This nigga even look good while he's eating.*

Perry chuckled. "Why are you looking at me like that? I got a booger in my nose or something?"

"No. I'm just sitting here wondering why a handsome man like yourself don't have a girlfriend or a wife."

"Because I'm very picky. A lot of women want me, I'm not going to lie, but I can tell if it's for all the wrong reasons or not."

"Oh really?" Diamond said sarcastically.

Perry smiled. "Really."

As Diamond spoke, Perry sized her up, and instantly he could tell that Diamond wasn't like the average woman. She seemed like a real and down-to-earth woman, and all that did was turn him on even more. "So what do you like to do for fun?"

"Anything that's fun." Diamond heard her cell phone ringing. She pulled it out of her purse, and when she saw Kendu's name flashing across the screen, she quickly sent him to her voice mail.

"Was that him?"

"Yes," Diamond said, keeping it real. She had no reason to lie, especially since she had already told him that she was married from the beginning.

"Well, I'm guessing you have to leave."

"Nah, I'm straight," Diamond said. "He'll be all right until I get there."

Perry laughed. He loved how Diamond carried herself. "So, after tonight, will I be able to see you again?"

Diamond smirked. "How you know if I even want to see you again?"

"Because I know you do." Perry sipped his orange juice.

"We'll see," Diamond replied as she finished up her food. "No promises, though."

"I can live with that." Perry dropped some bills on the table then stood up. "Let me get you back to your car before I get you killed."

Diamond sucked her teeth and rolled her eyes, but she knew that if she didn't get home soon she would definitely be in big trouble. More trouble than she was already in.

Perry pulled back up to the club, right next to Diamond's car. "So this is it for now, I guess"

"Yeah," Diamond said. "I definitely had a wonderful time with you tonight."

"The first of many."

Diamond smirked as she slid out the car. "Good night."

"Good night."

Perry watched her get in her car and pull off.

Diamond pulled into her driveway, and immediately she noticed that the living room light was on, which meant Kendu was still up. "I hope this nigga don't be on no bullshit when I get in there."

She stepped foot in the house and saw Kendu sitting at the kitchen table with a bottle of Grey Goose in front of him. "Hey, baby," she said as she hung up her jacket on the coat rack that stood by the door.

"Hey, baby, *my ass!*" Kendu snarled. "Where the fuck you been? And why the fuck you ain't answer the phone when I called you?"

"I went out to the club, and when you called me I didn't hear my phone ring." Diamond noticed blood on Kendu's shirt. "What happened to you?"

"All of our fuckin' money is gone," Kendu said in a low voice, his head hung low. Right now he was at his lowest point and didn't know what to do.

"Hold on, hold on," Diamond said as she sat down across from Kendu. "What you mean, all of our money is gone? And why is there blood on your shirt?"

"Carmen called me earlier. Somebody broke into her house, beat her half to death, and took all of our money." Kendu took a swig from the bottle. "They emptied out the whole safe."

Instantly Diamond felt stupid for being mad at him, but she just couldn't help herself. She'd automatically imagined Carmen and Kendu having sex. "How much did they take?"

"Sixty-nine thousand," Kendu replied, shaking his head.

"Damn! And you don't know who could've done this?"

"Nah, but I got a few cats in mind." Kendu took another swig. "I'ma get to the bottom of this, trust me."

"Anything I can do to help?"

"Yeah—Answer your muthafuckin' phone when I call you."

"You got it, daddy." Diamond grabbed his hand. "You know I'm here until the end, right?"

"Yeah, I know, baby." Kendu he kissed her hand. "But I am going to need you to slow down with the outrageous spending for a while until I get this shit back in order."

"Consider it done, baby," Diamond said. "Now let's get you upstairs and up out of these bloody clothes."

Upstairs she watched Kendu as he lay across the bed with an angry look on his face. She knew if he ever found out who was responsible for the robbery, he was definitely going to kill them. For the rest of the night Diamond lay in the bed with Kendu in complete silence. Not knowing what to say, she didn't want to upset him anymore than he already was.

Chapter 4

Kendu pulled up a block away from his trap house. He looked through his rearview mirror and saw Deuce pull up directly behind him. He slid out of his car looking over both shoulders as him, and Deuce walked around to the back door of the trap house. Kendu did the special knock, and seconds later a big strong-looking guy with a baby face answered the door.

"What's good, big homie?" The big man stepped to the side so Kendu and Deuce could enter.

"Where the fuck that nigga Spider at?" Kendu asked, looking around. This time things were in much better order and looked a lot more organized.

Seconds later Spider came trotting down the stairs with his pants hanging off his ass. "What's good, five?" he said, giving Kendu and Deuce some dap.

"I took a hit the other day," Kendu said. "Anybody heard anything about that?"

"I heard about what happened," Spider replied. "But I ain't heard shit about who was behind that shit."

"A'ight. Keep your ear to the streets for me."

"You know I got you, but for real, though"—Spider paused—"that shit sound like it was an inside job. I mean, who knew where your stash was?"

"Just me and Deuce."

Immediately all eyes were on Deuce.

"Fuck outta here!" Deuce said. "I was with Kendu all day that day. We were only apart for an hour, if that."

"He's right," Kendu quickly interjected. "Some hungry niggas was probably watching me, and I got caught slipping."

An hour was way more than enough time for Deuce to have kicked in Carmen's door and cleaned out his safe, but Kendu refused to let that thought even creep into his mind. Him and Deuce grew up together, so no way would, or could, his friend cross him like that.

"Shit been moving lately, though," Spider said, changing the subject. He handed Kendu a big wad of cash.

"That's what I'm talking about." Kendu quickly thumbed through the bills. "I'ma need you to stay on your grind," he said, giving Spider a pound.

Before Kendu could say another word, a young lookout came busting in through the front door. "Yo!" the lookout said in an out-of-breath voice, "Dirty Black just pulled up!"

Immediately a little bit of fear crept into Kendu's heart, but he had to hold it down, since his whole crew was watching him. "The nigga outside right now?" Kendu snatched his .45 from his waistband.

The lookout nodded his head yes, a scared look on his face.

Kendu cocked his .45 as he headed to the front door. He stepped outside and saw Dirty Black leaning on his silver Benz with a smirk on his face. Next to him stood a six-feet-seven monster whose whole body looked like it was one solid muscle, and across the street sat a car full of goons waiting for Kendu to act up, so they could have a reason to kill him.

Kendu walked up to Dirty Black with his .45 by his side, and Deuce a few steps behind him. "What's good?" Kendu asked, stopping a few feet away from Dirty Black.

"Put that muthafuckin' gun away before I take that shit and kill you with it!" The big man took two steps forward, making the muscles in his chest jump in the process.

Kendu looked across the street at the car full of goons and decided to do as he was told.

"Fall back, Amazon," Dirty Black said, calling the big man off.

"So what's up?" Kendu asked.

"What's up is, I came to collect the money you owe me." Dirty Black had already peeped all the traffic that Kendu's trap house was drawing.

Dirty Black favored the rapper Flavor Flav, except instead of a Vikings hat, he wore a brand-new Yankee fitted and a lot of jewelry, the same jewelry that kept him surrounded by beautiful women.

"What money?" Kendu said, acting dumbfounded.

"Nigga!" Dirty Black huffed. "Don't fuckin' play with me! You know exactly what I'm talking about. You took something from one of my workers that belonged to me. And I want it back."

"I just took a hit the other day and—"

"Not my problem," Dirty Black said, quickly cutting him off. "You got two months to come up with my money."

"Damn! Fifty grand in two months. That's a lot of money," Kendu said.

Immediately Dirty Black and Amazon busted out laughing.

"Fifty? Nah, nigga. You gotta pay another fifty just for taking it, and another fifty for me just letting you live, so the total is now one fifty."

"A $150 grand? How am I supposed to come up with that type of money in two months?"

"That's not my problem," Dirty Black said with a smirk on his face. "I'll be in touch." And he and Amazon slid back in the whip and peeled off.

"Fuck!" Kendu cursed loudly. He knew it would be damn near impossible for him to come up with that money in such a small space of time without him going to jail or being killed in the process.

"We gon' figure something out," Deuce said, feeling sorry for his partner.

"What we going to figure out?" Kendu snapped. "Basically I have two more months to live!"

"We just going to have to go extra hard out here in these streets." Deuce looked at Kendu for a response. He wished there was a way he could get the money for Kendu, but the reality was, it was going to be damn near impossible to get up that kind of money in such a short amount of time.

"I'ma holla at you later. I gotta go home and think." Kendu gave Deuce a pound and headed over towards his car.

"Please, don't do this. Please. I have a family!" the beautiful light-skinned woman begged.

Perry stood over her, shaking his head. In his hands he held an electrical saw. "Don't start begging now," he said, making the saw come to life.

"I have money!" she yelled out.

Perry smirked. "That's your problem. Y'all think because y'all have money and looks that can kill, you can do whatever and treat people however." He huffed as he placed some duct tape over her mouth then aimed the saw down at the woman's ankles. The woman's eyes got as big saucers when she felt the saw cutting through her ankle.

Once Perry got finished with the woman's ankles, he moved up to her knee caps. A smirk danced on his lips as the blood from the woman's legs splashed up on his face. "I'm sick and tired of you bitches acting as if y'all run the fuckin' world!" he said through clenched teeth.

Once Perry was done he pulled a straight razor from his pocket and carved the woman's face up like he did to all of his victims. "Bitch!" Perry growled as he walked over to the bath room and looked at his bloody face in the mirror. He just shook his head as he grabbed a washrag and slowly washed the blood from his face.

Diamond sat on the couch having herself a glass of wine as she watched the news. "What the fuck?" she said out loud as she heard the news report about another woman turning up dead with her face all sliced up. "Who the fuck just goes around cutting bitches up?" she thought out loud.

She took another sip of her wine as she heard Kendu coming through the front door. "Hey, baby," Diamond sang as she ran and met her husband at the door, her ass jiggling all the way to the door in her orange boy shorts and wife-beater.

"Hey, what's up?" Kendu hugged Diamond weakly.

"What's wrong, baby?" she asked, sensing something was wrong.

"The question is, what ain't wrong?" Kendu walked over to the kitchen table.

"Talk to me, baby. What's up?"

"That nigga Dirty Black came to pay me a little visit today." Kendu took Diamond's glass of wine and downed it. "Muthafucka talking about I got two months to pay him back $150 grand, when I only took fifty grand from him in the first place."

"What kind of shit is that?" Diamond asked, her face crumpled up. "So what we going to do?"

"It's only one thing we can do," Kendu said, massaging the bridge of his nose. "I'm going to have to kill Dirty Black."

"Oh my God!" Diamond sighed. "Baby, can't we just move?"

"Nah, we ain't moving nowhere, baby. I'm going to figure something out," Kendu told her.

Deep down inside Kendu didn't know what his next move was going to be. He knew it was going to be damn near impossible to get up the $150 grand in such a short amount of time, and he also knew that trying to kill Dirty Black would end up being just as hard. But at the end of the day, he knew he would have to do something. The question was, what?

"Don't worry, daddy. We'll come up with something. I'll get a job if you need me to."

"Nah, baby, I don't need you doing all that." Kendu went into deep thought. "I'll figure something out, like I always do."

"Well, whatever I have to do to help I'm going to do it." Diamond hated to see her husband worried. He said he had everything under control, but she knew his pride wouldn't allow him to ask for help.

"I'ma go upstairs and chill for a minute." Kendu poured himself a glass of wine before heading upstairs.

Once Kendu disappeared upstairs, Diamond grabbed the bottle of wine from the fridge and followed him upstairs.

"Take all that shit off!" she demanded, standing directly in front of Kendu.

Her aggressiveness forced him to crack a smile. "You got it, baby," he said, doing as he was told.

Diamond aggressively grabbed Kendu's dick and placed it in her mouth. She moaned like it was her first home-cooked meal in years. "You like that, daddy?" she asked, looking up in his eyes.

"Damn, baby!" Kendu groaned, looking down at her.

Diamond grabbed the wine bottle and poured some on his dick. She quickly slurped as much of it off as possible, as she sucked the shit out of his dick, moaning loudly the whole time.

After about ten minutes of that, Diamond quickly hopped up on her feet and bent over and grabbed her ankles. And Kendu smoothly eased up behind her and slid inside of her.

"Damn!" he moaned, sliding in and out of her wet walls, enjoying every second of it. When he felt himself getting ready to come, he sped up his strokes. Then as he pulled out, he grunted and came all over Diamond's ass. "Damn!" he said out of breath, flopping backwards on the bed.

"Who's the best?" Diamond asked with a smirk on her face as she headed to the bathroom to take a shower.

"You are, baby," Kendu said, his eyes closed.

Chapter 5

"Fuck!" Diamond cursed loudly as she slowed down for the yellow light. Ever since Kendu had told her about the situation with Dirty Black, that was all she could think about. She needed to find a way to help out her husband. She didn't know what she was going to do, but she knew she had to help out some kind of way.

She pulled into the parking lot of one of her favorite diners. All that thinking made her hungry. She hopped out her car and quickly entered the restaurant. Her mind was so all over the place, she didn't even know she was being followed.

Perry pulled in the parking spot next to Diamond's car, and let his engine die. He had been following her for the past two days, waiting for the perfect opportunity to pretend he was just bumping into her by accident. He quickly glanced at himself in the mirror before heading inside the diner.

As soon as he stepped in the diner, he immediately spotted Diamond sitting alone at a table, skimming through the menu. "Hey, I thought that was you sitting over here," Perry said with a smile. "What you doing up in here?"

"I come here all the time," Diamond replied. She nodded her head, signaling him to sit down. "The question is, what are *you* doing here?"

Perry looked at her like she was crazy. "I come here all the time," he lied. He quickly browsed through the menu. "It's nice to see you again. Next time I just hope it's not by accident."

Diamond smiled. "It's not like that. But you already know that I'm married."

"I mean, you not allowed to have friends?" he asked seriously.

"Yeah, I can have friends, but I don't really need any new friends right now. I have a lot on my mind right now, and would hate to be mean to you for no reason," she said honestly.

"Well, what's wrong?" Perry asked, hoping somehow he could help her out.

"Oh, it's nothing," Diamond answered quickly. She didn't want to tell him about her and her husband's money problems.

"I have a lot of connections," Perry told her. "You never know . . . I might be able to help."

Diamond thought about it for a second. She knew that in order to keep her husband alive and out of harm's way that somehow she had to help bring in some money.

The waiter walked up and interrupted her thoughts. "Are y'all ready to order?"

Perry looked over at Diamond. Once she ordered, he placed his order.

He pressed. "So are you going to tell me what's wrong?"

"Money!" Diamond said finally. "I need to find a way to make a few extra dollars."

Perry busted out laughing. "Is that all?"

"What's so funny?" Diamond asked, not finding anything funny about what she had just said.

"Oh, nothing. I just thought it was something a little more serious."

"Well, to me it is serious, real serious," Diamond said, rolling her eyes.

Perry stopped laughing. "Tell you what I can do. I can let you work at the club at nights, and I'll look out for you."

"What would I have to do?" she asked suspiciously. "And look out for me how?"

"The same thing everybody else does that works at the club." Perry smirked.

"Okay, but don't think just 'cause you hooking me up that I owe you anything, 'cause if that's the case, then you can take that job and shove it up your ass." Diamond meant every word she spoke.

"Let me tell you something," Perry said, leaning forward so Diamond could hear him. "Whatever I want, I can get, point-blank. All I'm trying to do is help. If you want it, you can take the job, if not, then you don't have to."

"Sorry. I'm just not used to people being so nice to me for nothing. Plus, I don't like for people to feel like I owe them anything, you feel me?"

"I totally understand, 'cause I'm the same way. All I'm trying to do is help a sister out. Whenever you ready, just give me a call." He handed her his business card.

"Thanks," Diamond said, accepting it. She knew that her getting a job wouldn't sit well with Kendu. "I enjoyed lunch with you, but I think I better get going."

"Yeah, it is getting pretty late. Make sure you give me a call."

"Yes, of course."

The two shook hands and went their own separate ways.

As Diamond walked off, Perry made sure he watched her nice-sized ass switch from side to side until she slid in her vehicle. "Damn!" he said to himself, as she pulled out into traffic. "I gotta have her."

Chapter 6

Kendu sat in his trap house with a stressed-out look on his face. A week had passed, and he still didn't have a plan on how he could come with even half of the money.

"You came up with anything yet?" Spider asked, stirring his vodka and orange juice.

"Nah, not yet. I'm having a hard time thinking. This shit is fuckin' with my brain."

"You might just have to leave town," Deuce suggested.

"And look like a coward?" Kendu huffed. "Fuck outta here! I'ma figure something out, like I always do."

No matter what, leaving town wasn't an option for Kendu. His pride and manhood just wouldn't allow him to go out like that. He had spent his whole life building up his street rep, and refused to let another man take what he'd worked so hard for. At the end of the day, Dirty Black was a man just like him.

"It's only one thing I can do," Kendu said, getting everyone's attention.

"And what's that?" Deuce asked.

"I'm gonna have to get the connect to front me a few extra bricks. And we going to have to get ruthless out here on these streets and hit 'em hard."

"What did you have in mind?" Deuce asked.

"Basically, if I don't come up with this money, I'm a dead man, so with that being said, whatever I gotta do, I'ma do. Shit, I ain't got shit else to lose."

"I'ma push these niggas as hard as I can," Spider said. "We going to get this money up for you."

"I appreciate it, my nigga." Kendu gave Spider a pound as he stood up to leave. "I'ma scream at y'all later." He gave everybody a pound then made his exit.

Kendu slid in his Acura and pulled away from his trap house, the sound of Jay-Z filling his car as he just drove around, thinking. "Fuck!" He cursed loudly, not knowing what his next move was going to be.

As Kendu pulled up at a red light, he saw Dirty Black and about thirty of his goons in the middle of the projects having a cookout. "Fuck this shit!" He quickly pulled over and hopped out his whip. He needed to have a word with Dirty Black, let him know what was on his mind.

"Nigga, I fucked seven bitches last night, all from the same family," Dirty Black was saying, causing everybody around him to bust out laughing.

Amazon's laughter quickly came to an end when he saw Kendu approaching. "Fuck you want?" he asked, blocking Kendu's path.

"I need to talk to Dirty Black for a second."

"Fuck you mean, you need to talk to Black for a second?" Amazon frowned. "Can't you see we busy taking care of the community right now?"

"It will only take a second."

"Muthafucka, didn't I just tell you"—Amazon growled as he roughly hemmed Kendu up—"that he's busy right now?"

"Let him go!" Dirty Black ordered.

Kendu fixed the collar of his shirt. "Yo', Black, I need to talk to you for a second."

"You got five minutes, so make it quick," Dirty Black said, a blunt dangling from his black lips.

"I'ma be straight up with you," Kendu said. "I'm going to need some more time to get up that money."

"No can do!" Dirty Black said quickly. "Didn't your mother ever tell you not to take things that don't belong to you? Now you gotta deal with the consequences."

"I didn't know it was your shit I was taking," Kendu told him. "I gets paper however I can. You gotta respect that."

A smirk danced on Dirty Black's lips. "I like your style, so I'll tell you what I'ma do for you." He paused to light up his blunt. "I'm going to let you work for me for a whole year for free."

"Damn? A whole year?" Kendu echoed.

"Listen, I'm trying to help you out. The choice is yours," Dirty Black said nonchalantly. "Take it or leave it."

"What I gotta do?"

"Whatever needs to be done," Dirty Black answered quickly. "You owe me, so you can either pay with your life or by working for me for a year. What's it going to be?"

"Give me a day or two to sleep on it," Kendu said.

"You got twenty-four hours to get back to me, fam." Dirty Black chuckled as he walked off, leaving Kendu standing there looking confused.

Perry sat upstairs in the club in his office counting money. He had a hard time trying to focus, because the only thing on his mind was Diamond, he loved how she carried herself. It was just something about her. Perry didn't know how, but he planned on stealing her away from her husband. He felt that if anybody deserved her, it was him.

His office phone grabbed his attention. "Hello," he answered.

"Yeah, it's this chick down here talking about she needs to speak with you, and she said it's important," the manager told him.

"A'ight, I'll be right down." After Perry hung up the phone, he grabbed the bottle of Ciroc that sat at the end of his desk and poured himself a quick shot and downed it. "I'm ready to go home," he said out loud, and headed downstairs.

Perry's face lit up when he reached the bottom of the steps and saw Diamond sitting at the end of the bar patiently waiting for him. "I hope I didn't have you waiting too long," he said in his sexiest voice.

"No, I wasn't waiting that long." Diamond smiled as she quickly gave him the once-over.

"What can I do for you?" Perry asked, placing both of his hands in the pockets of his slacks, a smile on his face.

"I'm here for the job." Diamond hated that she had to get a job, but for Kendu, there wasn't anything she wouldn't do.

"Let's go up to my office so we can talk."

Perry led the way up the steps, and Diamond followed him to his office.

Perry sat down behind his desk and poured two shots of Ciroc. "So why didn't you call me?"

"I had to throw your card away." Diamond accepted the drink he handed her. "If my husband found another man's card in my possession, he would kill me."

Perry chuckled. "I understand," he said, just happy that she was sitting in front of him at this very moment.

"So what you gon' have me doing up in this joint?" Diamond asked, looking around. "I ain't cleaning no toilets or no dumb shit like that, I'm telling you that now."

"Nah." Perry smiled. "You can work the bar if you like. That's really the only thing I'll have you doing up in here. You are way too beautiful to be working too hard up in here."

"That's nice and all that, but I got problems, so I gotta do what I gotta do."

"I understand." Perry downed his shot. "So when can you start?"

"Shit, tonight, if you need me to." Diamond laughed, but she was dead serious.

Perry smirked. "Tomorrow night will be fine."

"Okay, thanks. I appreciate everything you are doing for me."

"It's nothing," Perry said, looking at Diamond's titties on the low. They were sitting right there staring at him.

"Okay, so I guess I'll see you tomorrow," Diamond said, as she stood up to leave.

"Let me walk you to your car." Perry stood up. He grabbed Diamond's waist as he led her back down the steps, treating her like, if he let her go, she would break.

They reached the parking lot, and Diamond quickly removed her keys from her purse. "Thanks for everything."

"If you ever want to talk about your problem that you have, feel free. I'm always available, if ever you want to talk about it."

"I'll be all right, but thanks for being concerned." Diamond smiled as she slid behind the wheel of her whip. "I'll see you tomorrow."

"See you tomorrow," Perry said, looking at his watch. "Matter of fact, I have to run to the crib and take care of something myself." He waved bye and walked off to the other side of the parking lot and slid in his Range Rover.

***

Diamond pulled up to her home and saw Kendu's car in the driveway. She stepped in the crib and saw him sitting at the kitchen table. "Hey, baby."

"Where the fuck you been at?" Kendu growled.

"I was out with my friend Tiffany." Diamond was scared to tell him she went out and got a job to help him out.

"Why the fuck you ain't never home no more?"

"Well, I ain't gon' just sit up in the house all day while you out all day and night," she said, flipping the script on him. "You must got me fucked up."

"Watch your mouth!" Kendu warned with a point of his finger.

"Sorry, daddy," she said in apology. "Did you come up with a plan yet?"

"Not yet, but I'm working on something, as we speak."

"Are you going to let me know what it is?" Diamond asked as she heard a light knock at the door.

"That's Deuce." Kendu got up and answered the door.

"What's good, five?" Deuce said, giving Kendu a pound. "Hey, Diamond. How you feeling?"

"Hey, Deuce. I'm good." Diamond kissed Kendu on the lips. "I'ma go upstairs so y'all can talk." She turned and trotted up the steps.

Deuce helped himself to a seat at the kitchen table. "So what's popping?"

"Dirty Black told me if I couldn't pay him, I could work for him for free for a whole year," Kendu told him, waiting for a response.

"Damn! A whole year?"

"A whole year."

"You gon' do it?"

"I don't really have a choice," Kendu said, rubbing the bridge of his nose. "It's either that or get killed."

"Anything you need me to do?" Deuce asked.

"All I need you to do is go hard out here in the streets and make sure Spider and the rest of them niggas get that money."

"I got you. You just make sure you be careful. Dirty Black is a dirty muthafucka!"

Kendu smirked. "Yeah, I know."

Perry entered his home and made a beeline for his bedroom. He went straight to his closet and grabbed his all-blue mechanic suit, put it on over his outfit, and quickly headed down to the basement. In the basement sat a dark-skinned woman tied to a chair laying on its side. She had rocked back and forth so much in the chair, trying to escape, she had tipped the chair over on its side.

"I see someone has been being a bad girl," Perry said, a menacing smile on his face as he slipped his fingers in the latex gloves.

The woman tried to speak, but all that came out was muffled moans, due to the duct tape covering her mouth.

"I see I'm going to have to teach you a lesson." Perry grabbed the iron and plugged it into the socket. "One you won't forget."

The woman's eyes got as big as fifty-cent pieces as she struggled to get free, but it was no use. Perry watched the woman try her hardest to get free for fifteen minutes before he made his move.

The first thing he did was rip the her blouse straight off her back. He then grabbed the iron off the table and made his way toward her. "Is it hot in here, or is it me?"

He laughed at his own joke like it was the funniest shit he'd ever heard.

"Now this is going to hurt a little bit," he whispered. Then he pressed the iron on the woman's stomach for about four seconds.

The smell of burning flesh attacked his nostrils as he watched the skin from her stomach get stuck to the iron.

"You like that, don't you?" Perry pressed the iron on the woman's stomach once again, this time on the other side.

"Let's try the legs next," he said, smashing the iron down on the woman's leg. Then he worked his way on to the other leg, then the arms, then her back.

Perry then pressed the steaming hot iron on the woman's face and held it there. He listened to the flesh sizzle on the hot iron as he held it down on her face. After holding the iron down for over a minute, he removed it, along with half of the woman's face.

He then removed his razor from his pocket and went to work on what was left of her face. "You dirty-ass bitch!" he growled, slicing the woman's throat.

Kendu reached the location where Dirty Black and his crew hung out at and knocked on the door.

Seconds later some ugly black nigga answered the door. "Fuck you want?" he asked, a frown on his face.

"I'm here to see Dirty Black," Kendu replied, not in the mood to play around with the ugly man.

The ugly guy looked Kendu up and down. "Nah, fam. Ain't no Dirty Black here." The ugly guy tried to close the door.

But Kendu stuck his foot inside before it closed. "Yo', I don't got time to be playing. Tell that nigga Dirty Black that Kendu is out here to see him!"

The ugly guy looked at Kendu like he was crazy and swung on him, punching him on the side of his head. Kendu took the punch well and fired back with a quick two-piece. The two then went blow for blow, each one taking the next man's best punch.

"Yo', these niggas out in the hallway getting busy!" a young shooter announced, causing everybody to run in the hallway and watch the fight.

Dirty Black and the rest of his crew quickly rushed out into the hallway in time to see Kendu catch the ugly guy with one last punch before he dropped low and scooped his legs from up under him, then dumped him on his head, causing them to erupt in a loud "Ooooooooooh!"

"Yo', go break that shit up." Dirty Black nodded at Amazon.

Amazon got in between the two men and separated them with ease. "Y'all niggas chill the fuck out!" he boomed.

"I'ma kill you, muthafucka!" the ugly guy yelled, knowing Kendu got the better of him.

"Yo', chill the fuck out," Dirty Black said to the ugly guy. He walked over to Kendu and draped his arm over his shoulder. "I like how you handled that back there."

"I'm just here to get to business," Kendu stated plainly.

"Follow me," Dirty Black said with a smirk on his face.

Dirty Black knew he was getting over on Kendu, because the man was in a bind, and Dirty Black knew his crew was too strong for him to be touched. He sat behind his desk with a smile on his face.

"What's so funny?"

"Nothing." Dirty Black scribbled something down on a piece of paper and slid it to Kendu.

"What's this?"

"Some clown named Gansta Tone just got out of jail and call himself taking back his old block, which happens to belong to me now." Dirty Black paused. "I need you to get this muthafucka the fuck up off my corner, and I need you to do it quickly."

"A'ight, I got you," Kendu said as he stood up to leave.

"You need a ratchet?"

"Nah, I got heat," Kendu replied as he made his exit.

"Holla at me when that's done." Dirty Black watched Kendu make his exit. He knew Gansta Tone didn't play, so this job was a test to see exactly what Kendu was made of. If he failed, then that would cost him his life, and if he passed, he just lived another day to complete another mission.

Chapter 7

Diamond entered the empty club and immediately spotted Perry, talking to a few employees.. She knew she had no business working in the nightclub, but her husband's life depended on it, or at least she thought it did.

"Hey, what's up?" Perry asked with a smile on his face.

"Ready to get to work," Diamond replied, looking around.

"Good. 'Cause it's going to be packed up in here tonight."

"So what you need me to do?"

"Basically take orders at the bar. If you need any help, Monica will help you." He nodded over at the light-skinned woman who stood behind the bar. "Just relax. You're gonna do fine."

"Okay, no problem," Diamond said as she walked over and joined Monica behind the bar. She didn't have a clue, but she planned on doing the best she could.

Kendu cruised past the block that Gansta Tone was supposed to be on. Immediately he spotted the Spanish man with long braids that came down to the middle of his back. Gansta Tone stood on the block with a few of his workers, and just by looking at him Kendu could tell that the man didn't play no games, and was about his business. The way his team flocked around him told Kendu that Gansta Tone was a powerful man. This job wasn't going to be as easy as he thought it would be.

Kendu parked his car about a block away from where Gansta Tone and his crew stood. He quickly loaded his .45 and tossed his hood on the top of his head as he slid out of his car.

Gansta Tone sat, leaned up against his Escalade, talking to his workers, when he noticed a man wearing a hoody walking swiftly in their direction. "Yo', who this right here?" he asked, his hand immediately sliding to his waistline.

Kendu noticed how Gansta Tone and his crew tensed up as he approached. "Fuck!" He cursed under his breath as he walked past Gansta Tone and his crew and headed inside the building. "Fuck it!" he said to himself. He would just have to wait until Tone and his crew came into the building.

Two hours later Kendu saw Tone finally making his way towards the building. "About fuckin' time." He pulled out his .45 and waited.

"Yo', I'll be right back," Tone said as he headed towards his building. "I gotta go upstairs and finish bagging up. Y'all niggas, hold it down out here until I get back."

Tone reached his building and popped open the door. He entered the building, and before he could turn the corner, he saw the barrel of a .45 in his face.

"What the fuck!?" Gansta Tone growled before he saw the muzzle on the gun flash and heard a loud *BOOM!*

Kendu watched Tone's body drop to the ground as blood and brains splattered all over the mailbox and wall. As soon as Tone's body hit the ground, he exited the building, running full speed. Next thing you know, he heard gunshots ringing out. He looked up and saw Gansta Tone's crew shooting at him. He immediately returned fire before hopping over the fence and making his getaway on foot, leaving the stolen car he'd come in.

"Thanks, girl for helping me out tonight," Diamond said. The night ended up being harder than she expected.

"Don't mention it, girl," Monica replied. "I think you did pretty good for your first day."

"Yeah, give me about a week, and I'll have this whole thing mapped out." Diamond grabbed her jacket as she got ready to leave.

"Okay, girl, I'll see you tomorrow."

As soon as Diamond stepped foot in the parking lot, she heard footsteps coming from behind her. She quickly turned around and grabbed her heart in relief when she saw it was only Perry. "Don't sneak up on me like that. You scared the shit outta me," she said with a smile.

"My bad. You know I gotta make sure you get to your car safe," he said. "So how did you like your first day?"

"It was cool. My feet hurt."

"Well, maybe you should let me rub them one day." Perry stepped in way closer than he needed to be.

"That's why I have a husband," Diamond replied with a smirk. She hopped behind the wheel of her car. "See you tomorrow." She waved as she pulled out of the parking lot, leaving Perry standing there.

Perry stood in the parking lot and watched Diamond pull off. His patience was running thin. He had to have Diamond and soon. It was just something about her that made her different from all the other arrogant women that he'd killed for no reason. Perry knew he had a sick problem, but for some strange reason he felt that she might be the one to help him with it. He just felt, with Diamond on his side, nothing else mattered.

Diamond pulled into her driveway and quickly exited her vehicle and headed inside the house. She was tired, and just wanted to hop in the shower and go straight to sleep. She walked in the door and was startled when she saw Kendu sitting at the table with blood on his shirt.

"Oh my God! Baby, are you all right?" She rushed over to Kendu's side.

"Bitch, where the fuck you been at all night?" Kendu barked. "It's muthafuckin' four o'clock in the morning."

Diamond said the first thing that came to her mind. "I—I—I was at the club."

Kendu quickly shot up from his seat and forcefully grabbed her throat and pushed her backwards until her back hit the wall. "Don't fuckin' play with me!" He growled. "You don't even have on your club clothes, so where the fuck you been? And don't lie!"

"Get your fuckin' hands off of me!" Diamond struggled to loosen up his grip. "Muthafucka, when you coming up in here at muthafuckin' five o'clock in the morning, do I fuckin' question you to death? NO! So get your fuckin' hands off of me!"

Kendu looked dead in Diamond's face, smirked, then went out the door.

Immediately Diamond followed him to the door. "Yeah, that's right. Go run to your other bitches. You dirty muthafucka, this marriage is over! You never loved me in the first place!" she screamed, standing in the doorway. "You go run over those other bitches, not me!" she yelled as she slammed the door.

"Dirty-dick muthafucka!" She slouched down to the floor and put her knees in her chest and just cried. All she wanted to do was help her husband. She didn't understand why he talked to or treated her the way he did. After a while, Diamond got up, went upstairs, and just cried for the rest of the night.

Carmen looked through her peephole and saw Kendu standing on the other side of the door, she immediately opened the door and stepped to the side so he could enter. "Hey, baby. Everything all right?" Carmen kissed Kendu on the lips.

"Me and Diamond just had a big-ass fight. I'ma need to stay here for a few nights." Kendu plopped down on the couch.

"I hope y'all wasn't fighting over me again," Carmen said, feeling bad about interfering in their marriage. She knew it was wrong to be seeing a married man, but the feelings she had were too strong for her to stop.

"Nah. I think she cheating on me." Kendu was hoping he was wrong, but his gut told him different.

"Why would you say something like that?" Carmen asked with a concerned look on her face. Her face was healing very nicely after the brutal beating she took.

"Every time I come home now she's never there anymore. Then when I ask her where she was, she lies to me," he said in a defeated voice. He may have cheated on Diamond every once in a while, but Diamond was his life, and without her he felt totally incomplete and out of place.

"Just because she's not home when you get there doesn't mean that she's cheating on you," Carmen told him.

"Well, it means something. People just don't up and change out the blue."

"You may just need to talk to her, and try making a little more time for her," Carmen suggested.

"Fuck that!" Kendu said, waving her off. "She know what's going on out here in the streets. She know that I was on borrowed time. It's not like I want to be in the streets. I have to be in them, and now that this clown got me working for him, ain't no telling how much I'ma have to be out in the streets."

"I understand, because you talk to me about these things. Maybe you should talk to her about this situation."

"I'll think about it." Kendu massaged the bridge of his nose. He had so much on his mind and so much going on—pushing Diamond to the side and not even realizing it. Now it was too late because she was already sleeping with another man.

Chapter 8

Kendu pulled up to the block that Dirty Black and his crew hung out at and parked his car. It had been a month since he had last spoken to Diamond, and inside it was killing him. Ever since that day she didn't answer any of calls. And every time he went home, she was never there. Kendu walked up and gave Dirty Black a pound.

"What's good, *B*? How you feeling today?" Dirty Black asked, foam cup in his hand.

"I'm good," Kendu replied. "What's the plan for today?" he asked, needing something to take his mind off of Diamond.

"It's a light day today," Dirty Black told him. "I just need you and Amazon to go uptown and pick up some money from this clown named White Mike."

"That's it?"

"Then after that we gon' go get our party on downtown at this new club," Dirty Black said.

"Come on, nigga. Let's go get this shit over with, 'cause I got other shit I gotta do," Amazon said, and him and Kendu hopped in the all-black Yukon.

Amazon pulled up in front of White Mike's house and let the engine die. "You ready?" He turned and looked at Kendu.

"Let's do it," Kendu replied as he hopped out the truck.

Kendu reached the front door, and just as he got ready to knock, Amazon quickly kicked the front door open.

White Mike jumped up off the couch when he heard his front door get kicked in. He quickly grabbed the shotgun that rested under his couch, thinking it was the cops coming to arrest him. Once he saw Amazon pointing a .357 in his direction, he lowered his shotgun. "What's up, Amazon? My bad. I thought you was the cops."

"Dirty Black needs his money," Amazon said, never taking his eyes or gun off White Mike.

"I'm going to need at least another month," White Mike told him. "I just had to pay my lawyers a grip to get me up outta jail. Tell Dirty Black I got him, though. He knows I'm good for it."

Amazon didn't reply. Instead, he shot White Mike in his hand, causing him to drop his shotgun.

"Awwwww fuck!" White Mike screamed as he dropped down to his knees, clutching his hand.

White Mike's wife came running from upstairs when she heard the loud gunshot go off. "Oh my God!" she screamed, running and kneeling by her husband's side.

"I know you got some money up in here somewhere," Amazon growled as he walked over and stepped on White Mike's bloody hand with his Timberland boots.

"I swear I don't got shit up in here," White Mike pleaded.

"Oh, I know you got something up in here." Amazon looked over at White Mike's wife. "Yo', hold this nigga down," he said over his shoulder.

Immediately Kendu walked over toward White Mike, his .45 aimed directly at the man's face.

"Bitch, get ya ass up!" Amazon barked. He snatched White Mike's wife up off the floor by her hair. "Where the fuckin' money at?"

"I swear to God, I don't know nothing about no money."

Amazon sighed loudly as he pulled a Rambo knife from the small of his back and started stabbing the woman like she was an animal.

Kendu watched in horror as Amazon plunged the knife in and out of the woman repeatedly. White Mike tried to jump up and rescue his wife, but Kendu quickly erased that thought with a blow to the head with his gun.

Amazon stabbed White Mike's wife to death and kept on stabbing away.

Kendu grabbed his arm. "I think that's enough!" he said in a stern voice.

Amazon looked at Kendu like he was crazy. "Get your muthafuckin' hands off me before you be next!"

Kendu released his grip on Amazon's arm.

Amazon cleaned his Rambo knife off on Kendu's shirt. "Take care of this clown, so we can go."

Kendu turned and looked down at White Mike, who was holding his bloody hand. He felt sorry for the man, but he knew he had to do what he had to do. It was either kill or be killed. He raised his arm and shot White Mike in the face, and him and Amazon walked out like nothing never happened.

Amazon and Kendu got back to the hood, and Kendu listened to Amazon laugh, bragging about how he had viciously stabbed White Mike's wife to death. Kendu had done dirt in his day, but it was always a business move. Amazon was just a straight animal. He killed just for fun and for a street reputation, and from listening to him tell the story, he enjoyed doing it.

"This nigga Kendu was acting like he was scared to shoot that white nigga. The nigga hand was shaking more than Muhammad Ali," Amazon said, and him and the rest of the crew busted out laughing.

"All that matters is, I got the job done," Kendu countered.

"Everything all right?" Dirty Black asked. "You been kind of quiet these last couple of days."

"Yeah, I'm cool," Kendu replied.

"Let me talk to you outside for a second."

Dirty Black and Kendu stepped outside so they could talk in private.

"Talk to me. What's bothering you?" Dirty Black asked.

"I'm straight," Kendu lied.

"Listen, fam. Let me tell you something," Dirty Black began. "You on my team now, so if you have a problem, come to me and I'll take care of it."

"Just been having a little trouble with my wife." Kendu sighed loudly. "I think she fuckin' another nigga."

"You need him killed?" Dirty Black asked seriously.

"Not really certain yet if she's creeping or not."

"What does your gut tell you?"

"She fuckin'," Kendu answered seriously. And his gut was always right.

"It's a million women out here, fam." Dirty Black reached down in his pocket and peeled off five thousand dollars and handed it to Kendu. "Here. That's for your pockets."

"Good looking," Kendu said as he gratefully accepted the money.

"We headin' to the club in about thirty minutes, so get your head together. Have a few drinks and enjoy the night," Dirty Black said as he went back inside.

When Kendu had first started working with Dirty Black, he thought he was just another fool with money. But after working with the man, he learned that Dirty Black was one of the realest people he had ever met in his whole life. Even though he was told that he would have to work for free, Dirty Black was still paying him for every job he did, and always made sure he was good and felt like family.

Chapter 9

Dirty Black and his crew stepped up in the club thirty-deep, looking like stars. One of the bouncers quickly escorted him and his crew towards the VIP section. "Loosen up, fam," Dirty Black whispered in Kendu's ear as he patted him on the back.

"I'm good," Kendu yelled over the loud music. "I'll be right back. I gotta pee." He snaked his way through the crowd, headed to the restroom.

Diamond stood behind the bar serving drinks when she spotted someone who looked just like Kendu headed towards the restroom. "Nah, that ain't him," she told herself as she continued to serve drinks.

Five minutes later she saw the same man reappear from the restroom, and she couldn't believe her eyes. It was Kendu. "Oh my God! What the fuck is he doing here?" Diamond said out loud as she watched him disappear in the crowd.

Kendu made it back to the VIP section and noticed that they were half-naked women everywhere.

"Yo', Kendu, let me introduce you to somebody," Dirty Black said, draping his arm around him. "This here is Chocolate," he said, introducing Kendu to the fine, sexy, dark-skinned woman.

"Oh, you ain't tell me your friend was this fine." Chocolate backed Kendu into his seat then slid down on his lap.

"Take it easy on my man." Dirty Black winked at Chocolate and walked off.

Kendu let his hand slide down on Chocolate's ass as he went in. "So what's goody?"

"You tell me, baby," Chocolate countered, massaging Kendu's package through his jeans, working him into stiffness. "I'm down for whatever." She seductively licked her lips.

"We gon' make moves when we get up outta here," Kendu said, checking her out from head to toe.

Wocka Flocka's song, "O Let's Do It," came blaring through the speakers, and the club went crazy. Kendu saw every gang sign in America thrown in the air when that song came on.

"I'm about to go get me another drink. You want one?" he asked.

"Yeah. I'll take the same thing you having," Chocolate replied. She watched Kendu walk over towards where Dirty Black and the rest of the crew stood.

"How Chocolate over there treating you?" Dirty Black smiled, sitting between two women like a sandwich.

"She good, money," Kendu replied with a smile. For once in a long time he was having a good time. "I need some more drinks."

"Hold on. My man bringing back more ice right now." Dirty Black told him.

Seconds later a scrawny kid with a neck full of "Blood beads" entered the VIP section carrying a bucket of ice, his eyes low.

"Took you long enough, muthafucka!" Amazon yelled over the loud music.

"My bad, my bad," the scrawny kid said. "It's this fine-ass bitch behind the counter I was tryin'a bag," the kid said, motioning his head towards the bar. "And she got a fat ass."

"Damn! She is fine as a muthafucka," Amazon said, grabbing his crotch. "I'd tear that pussy up." He laughed loudly as he gave the scrawny kid some dap, and the two men laughed extra loudly.

Kendu looked over toward the bar and immediately spotted Diamond behind the counter serving drinks. *What the fuck is she doing up in here?* he thought to himself. "Y'all hold that down. That's my wife," he said, leaving the VIP section and heading straight for the bar.

Diamond handed a woman her drink, and when she looked up, she saw Kendu coming straight towards her. She had thought about hiding, but it was too late. He had already spotted her.

Kendu walked right up to the counter. "Fuck you doing up in here?" he yelled over the music.

"What does it look like I'm doing?" she shot back. "I work here."

"What you mean, you work here? Fuck you doing working up in here?" he said, looking around.

"We need money, right?" Diamond sucked her teeth with an attitude. "I'm just trying to help."

"What?" Kendu, his face crumpled, walked behind the counter so he could be face to face with his wife. "Didn't I tell you I had everything under control?"

"You always say that," Diamond said in a bored tone.

Kendu quickly smacked the shit outta Diamond, causing her to stumble back into the cash register. "Fuck you think you talking to like that?" he barked as he moved in closer.

Before he could even say another word, he felt some-body tapping him on his shoulder. He turned around and found himself face to face with a dark-skinned brother.

"I'm the owner of this club," Perry said in a profes-sional manner. "Is there a problem over here?"

"I'm talking to my wife right now! Mind your busi-ness!" Kendu said, turning his back to Perry.

"Anything in this club is my business!" Perry said in a firm tone.

Kendu turned around and looked at Perry like he was insane as he cocked back and punched him in the face. Before Perry could react, Kendu was all over him, trying to take his head off.

Perry hit the floor, and as Kendu was about to stomp him out, a big bouncer threw him in a choke hold, as several big bouncers moved in for the kill. Kendu struggled to get free as he saw one of the bouncers about to punch him with brass knuckles on.

As soon as the bouncer got close, Dirty Black smacked him in the head with a Hennessy bottle. Amazon dropped the bouncer who held Kendu in a choke hold with a punch to the back of his head. From there the brawl popped off. Amazon was dropping anybody in his path, women included, while the rest of the crew and the bouncers got busy.

Seconds later, the dirty guy that Kendu had a fight with on his first day pulled out a 9 mm and pumped four shots into the ceiling—*Pow! Pow! Pow! Pow!*—causing everybody to get low and scramble for their life.

Kendu looked around for Diamond, but he didn't see her. So he stayed low and ran up out the club.

***

"You all right?" Monica asked, helping Diamond up from off the floor.

"Yeah, I'm fine." Diamond quickly rushed over to Perry's side. He was bleeding from his nose, and he also had a cut on the corner of his eye. "Are you all right?"

"Yeah, I'm straight," Perry said, touching his eye. He just shook his head when his hand came away bloody. "You know that guy?"

"Yeah, that was my husband," Diamond said, embarrassed. "I'm so sorry about this."

Perry stood up and saw that the whole party had been shut down, and the only people still in the club were his staff and the DJ.

"Here. Let me help you clean that." Diamond tried to clean Perry's wounds with a wet napkin.

Perry quickly caught her hand in mid-air before the napkin touched his skin. "You had anything planned for when you got off work?"

"No," Diamond answered quickly. "Why? What's up?"

"Can you come with me to my crib real quick? I'ma need you to help count some money, unless you have to get home." Perry winced in pain, hoping to win Diamond's sympathy.

"Yeah, I can do that. Ain't like I can go home tonight anyway."

Perry stepped out in the parking lot just happy to be able to spend some quality time with Diamond. He didn't mind shedding a little of blood to be with his soon-to-be girl. "Follow me."

"Okay," Diamond replied. "And don't be driving all crazy."

***

"What the fuck was that back there?" Dirty Black asked when the whole crew got back to their chill spot.

"My bad," Kendu apologized. "When that clown hopped in my face, my first reaction was to snuff the nigga."

"Ain't nothing wrong with that," Amazon said from the sideline. "I do it all the time."

"That was your wife back there?" Dirty Black asked.

"Yeah."

"Fuck ya wife doing working at a club?" Dirty Black asked.

"She was trying to help me get up the money to pay you off." Kendu felt bad for overreacting. All Diamond was trying to do was help him out. "We had a fight before I could tell her that me and you had worked everything out."

"Listen, I know this is none of my business," Amazon said, jumping back into the conversation, "but that nigga who jumped in ya business was acting like he was more than your wife's boss . . . I'm just saying."

"Word? You think so?" Kendu asked seriously.

"Yeah, I saw the same shit," Dirty Black told him. "You might wanna look into that."

"Yeah, I think I'm gonna do that," Kendu said. Amazon and Dirty Black had just made his relationship with Diamond a lot more complicated just by stating their opinion. "Yo', I'm about to run to the crib and get this shit straight. I'ma holla at y'all tomorrow." He gave the whole crew dap before he headed home so he could get things straight with his wife.

"Well, this is it," Perry said as him and Diamond stepped foot inside his baby mansion.

By the look on Diamond's face, he could tell that she was feeling his crib.

"You like it?"

"Of course, I do. Perry, this house is beautiful," Diamond said, sounding like a little girl.

"Yeah, right. I know your crib is probably real nice."

"It is, but it ain't like this," Diamond said honestly.

"Let me give you a tour of the place," Perry said, leading the way.

Diamond followed Perry around his house with an amazed look on her face. Perry's crib was the bomb. He never had to leave his house if he didn't want to, because he had everything he could ever want inside.

"Where does this door lead to?" she asked, noticing that Perry forgot to show her what was behind one door in the house.

"Oh, umm, that's the basement," Perry said, fumbling for words.

"Can I see it? I know it probably looks like another little house down there."

"I would love to show you my basement, but I just had a flood down there the other day, and it's looking real nasty down there," he lied. "Once I get all that taken care of, I'll gladly give you a tour and show you around down there."

"No problem," Diamond said as the two sat down on the couch.

"Okay, I guess we can get down to business and start counting up this money."

"Hold up!" Diamond said in a stern voice. "We not counting shit until I take care of these cuts on your face." She stormed off to the bathroom.

A smile quickly spread across Perry's face. He loved that Diamond was such a real woman. Any other woman would have just helped count up the money, got paid and left, but not Diamond. She was so different in Perry's eyes.

Diamond returned from the bathroom carrying a washcloth and some peroxide. Perry sat back on the couch and watched as Diamond gently cleaned his wounds. With each wound she cleaned, Perry could feel the love.

"How you feel?" Diamond asked once she was done.

"Much better now." Perry walked over to the fridge and returned carrying a bottle of wine and a corkscrew. "I need a drink." He popped open the bottle and took a swig straight from it.

"Thanks for coming to my rescue back there."

"I would never let nobody hurt you. I don't care who they are." He handed Diamond the bottle.

Diamond could feel the chemistry between the two, so she immediately broke eye contact and changed the subject. "You ready to count this money?"

Perry stood up and walked over to the counter in the kitchen, from where he grabbed the book bag. He then returned back to the couch.

"Damn! You trying to have me counting all—"

Before Diamond could even finish off her sentence, Perry had leaned over and kissed her.

Diamond knew that what was going on was wrong, but she kissed him back anyway. She lay back on the couch as Perry slid in between her legs, and the two continued to kiss passionately.

Perry darted his tongue in and out of Diamond's mouth as he began to unbutton her pants. She watched as he removed her pants from around her ankles. When he tried to take off her thong, she lifted up, so he could pull them down easily. Her thong was soaking wet with her juices.

Once Perry spread Diamond's thighs apart, his eyes lit up when he saw how wet her pussy was. Immediately he dove in head first, gently holding her lips apart with his thumbs as he began licking her pussy like he was a kitten. Diamond threw her head back in ecstasy as she closed her eyes while loud moans escaped her lips.

Perry slipped two fingers in Diamond's warm, wet pussy as he licked and sucked all over her clit, giving it a nice spit-shine. After he made her come twice, he was ready to see how that pussy felt. He quickly stood up and scooped her up in his arms. As he carried her upstairs to the master bedroom, the two kissed nonstop until they reached the bedroom.

Diamond lay on her back in the bed with her legs spread wide open, playing with her clit with one hand, and holding one of her breasts in her mouth with the other hand.

Perry got butt naked, put a condom on, then crawled in the bed on top of her.

"No, wait. I want to ride you." She pushed him over and rolled on top of him then reached back and slipped him inside of her. "Damn!" she moaned as she started bouncing up and down on Perry's dick, loving every inch of him.

Perry gripped both of Diamond's ass cheeks and spread them open as she continued to ride him like she was riding a racehorse.

He finally exploded in the condom. "Damn, baby!" he said, breathing heavily. "You the best."

"I know." Diamond smiled as she lay her head on Perry's chest.

"Listen," Perry said, looking in her eyes, making sure he had her attention, "I know you got a lot going on right now, but I just want you know that I'll always be here for you."

"Thanks, Perry. I appreciate that," she said sincerely.

Diamond knew what she was doing wasn't right, but after spending so much time with Perry, she started to really like him. Plus, she refused to just sit around while Kendu just fucked everything walking.

For the rest of the night they just lay in the bed talking, until they fell asleep.

Kendu sat up all night waiting for Diamond to walk through the front door. The longer he sat up waiting, the more he thought about her out fucking another man, the angrier he became. He understood that she just wanted to help him out financially, but it was the way he had to find out that really hurt him. He'd rather her just come to him and talk to him, instead of going behind his back and getting a job, especially a job where everybody could see her.

The sun had come up, and Diamond still hadn't come home yet. Kendu continued to get his drink on as he continued to wait.

Once noon arrived, he came to the conclusion that she wasn't coming home no time soon. Deep down inside, he really just wanted to speak to his wife and let her know how he really felt. Not to mention, he was beginning to get a little worried about her safety and whereabouts. Even if she did stay out all night, she should've definitely been home by noon.

"Let me see what this nigga Deuce is up to," he said to himself. He pulled out his cell phone and dialed Deuce's number.

"So you sure only one person inside is strapped?" Mousey asked Deuce as they sat staked out across the street from Kendu's trap house, which the two had been keeping a close eye on for the past two weeks.

"Positive," Deuce replied. "Only nigga in there holding is Spider."

Mousey had been planning this hit for the past two weeks, and he felt today was the perfect day to execute his plan. He hated that Kendu was doing better than he was. To make matters worse, Kendu had teamed up with Dirty Black.

"How much money you said be up in there again?" Mousey asked, a greedy look in his eyes.

"About ten to fifteen thousand. Today is pickup day," Deuce answered quickly, knowing the routine like the back of his hand.

Mousey nodded his head then pulled out his Nextel and ordered his goons to run up inside the trap house.

"You promised nobody was going to get hurt," Deuce reminded him.

"Yo', relax," Mousey told him. "Ain't nobody going to get hurt. They just gon' go in there, take the money, then leave," he lied.

Before Deuce could reply, he heard his cell phone ringing. He looked at his phone and saw Kendu's name flashing across the screen. "Yo', what's good?" he answered.

"What you getting into today?" Kendu asked.

"Nothing. About to head over to the spot and pick that up," Deuce said, speaking in code.

"A'ight, bet. After you do that, holla at me. I have to talk to you about something."

"A'ight, I got you," Deuce said, ending the call.

As soon as he hung up the phone, he watched four of Mousey's goons kick in the front door of the trap house and bum-rush the joint. All he could do was pray that nobody got hurt.

***

Spider sat on a milk crate making sure the count was straight, counting twenty after twenty. "Damn, *B*! My fuckin' hands hurt." He got up and headed towards the kitchen so he could wash his hands. The money he'd been counting was dirty and smelled like shit.

After he washed his hands, he heard a loud boom come from the front door. "What the fuck!" he said out loud, pulling his 9 mm from his waist. Spider was ready to toss the gun, thinking it was the police coming to raid the place, but when he saw men wearing hoodies, he immediately aimed and opened fire as he backpedaled out the back door, popping shot after shot.

Mousey and Deuce sat in the car chilling when they heard a series of loud gunshots ring out.

"Fuck!" Deuce knew the plan wasn't going down as smoothly as they had planned. "What's going on in there?"

"How the fuck am I supposed to know?" Mousey replied, an evil smirk on his face.

Just as Deuce was about to say something else, he saw Spider run from behind the house and hop over the fence leading to the neighbor's backyard.

Once Mousey saw his goons exit the house, he immediately pulled off.

"What the fuck!" Deuce yelled. "You said nobody was going to get hurt!"

Mousey pulled over and put the car in park. "Listen, you punk muthafucka, this shit we do ain't for the weak. Understand? You gotta be a wolf to survive out here!"

"I *am* a wolf," Deuce told him. "Let me start killing people you grew up with, and we'll see how much of a wolf you are."

"Listen, I ain't mean for shit to go bad back there, but if we want the title, we going to have to take it! Ain't nobody just going to give it to us. If you ain't ready for that, let me know now." Mousey tried to make it seem like him and Deuce was in it together, but, really, all he cared about was himself and taking over. Deuce was just a pawn on his chessboard.

"I'm ready for whatever," Deuce said, and he just sat back and enjoyed the rest of the ride.

Kendu pulled up on the corner where Dirty Black said he would be. When he pulled up, he saw about thirty goons standing on the corner.

"What's good, my nigga?" He gave Dirty Black and Amazon a pound.

"Everything good," Dirty Black replied. "You patch everything up at home?"

"Nah, she never came home," Kendu said, an embarrassed look on his face.

"She'll be back," Dirty Black said as he draped his arm around Kendu's shoulder. "There's a million chicks out here, and I can get you anyone you want. It's nothing."

"Nah, I'm good," Kendu said, declining Dirty Black's offer. "I'm just focused on getting this money right now." Instead of worrying about what Diamond was out doing, Kendu decided to just get his money up. If she really loved him, then she would be back, or so he hoped.

"Cool," Dirty Black said, getting down to business. "I got another little job I need you to handle for me."

"What's up?"

Kendu, Dirty Black, and Amazon all walked away from the crowd.

"This clown Marcus caught some out-of-town niggas slipping last week. Word is, he held out on some of the money," Dirty Black explained.

"Hold on, hold on," Kendu said, confused. "If Marcus is the one who robbed the niggas, then why we paying him a visit?"

"I have a drug team, a stickup boys team, and I have a team that collects." Dirty Black smiled. "Marcus is on my stickup boys team, and you on my collect team, and I need you and Amazon to go collect that money he held out on."

"I guess." Kendu heard his cell phone ringing and quickly snatched it out the case, hoping it was Diamond calling him. When he looked at his phone and saw Deuce's number flashing across the screen, he answered with a slight attitude. "Yeah, what's up?"

"Yo', somebody just hit up the spot!" Deuce yelled into the phone, pretending to be shocked.

"Fuck you mean, somebody hit up the spot?" Kendu growled. "Where you at right now?"

"Two blocks away from the spot."

"I'm on my way!" Kendu said, hanging up in Deuce's ear.

"Everything all right?" Dirty Black asked.

"Yeah, everything good," Kendu said as he turned to face Amazon. "You ready to go handle this?"

Amazon didn't reply. Instead, he went and hopped in the passenger seat of the car. Kendu hopped in the driver's seat and pulled away from the curb like a madman. "Yo', I gotta make a stop real quick," he said as he made a quick detour.

For the entire ride Kendu racked his brain trying to figure out who had caught him slipping twice. He was so angry, he didn't even realize he had just run a red light.

"Yo', slow the fuck down," Amazon huffed, giving him a stern look.

"My bad," Kendu apologized.

When Kendu pulled up on the block, he saw police cars and flashing lights everywhere. "Fuck," he whispered as he cruised by slowly.

"Ain't that your spot?" Amazon asked, a smirk on his face.

"Yeah," Kendu replied dryly. He spotted Deuce's car and pulled over. "Give me a second." He hopped out the car and walked over to Deuce's car.

Deuce slid out the car and held his hand out for some dap.

"What happen?" Kendu said bluntly, leaving Deuce hanging.

"I pulled up and saw cops crawling all over the place," Deuce lied.

"You ain't heard nothing from Spider?"

"Nah, I ain't heard shit."

"Find out who was behind this before the night is out." Kendu turned and headed back to his car, leaving Deuce standing there.

"So it's like that?" Deuce yelled out, not liking the way Kendu spoke to him.

"Muthafucka!" Kendu growled as he walked back over to Deuce. "Nigga, you suppose to be on top of all this shit! Where the fuck was you at when all this shit went down?"

"I was on my way up here," Deuce lied again.

"You slipping. Whoever did this was the same muthafuckas who hit up Carmen's spot as well. They watching us."

"How you figure?" Deuce asked.

"Fuck you mean, how I figure? Open your fuckin' eyes!"

Kendu walked back over to his car and slid behind the wheel and pulled off.

Deuce stood there and watched as Kendu pulled off. He felt bad for what he was doing, but at the end of the day, it was every man for himself, and he wasn't about to be the one who got left out while everybody else ate. Kendu wasn't feeding him enough to get full, so he planned on doing what he had to do, and if that meant taking him out, so be it.

Amazon looked over and saw that Kendu had something on his mind. "What that clown was talking about?"

"A whole lot of nothing," Kendu said in a disgusted tone. "This the second time we done got hit, and he don't know shit."

"That's 'cause he probably the nigga who's robbing you," Amazon said with a raised eyebrow.

"Nah, I grew up with Deuce," Kendu said, quickly erasing the thought from his mind. He couldn't see Deuce doing something like that, especially after all the stuff the two had been through together.

"All I'm saying is, keep a eye on that clown. If he's in charge while you away, then everything falls on his shoulders, and he should be held accountable."

"I'ma get to the bottom of this," Kendu said as he pulled up in front of Marcus's building.

Kendu and Amazon quickly exited the car and made their way inside the building. Amazon reached the door and banged on it like he was the police.

Seconds later they heard feet shuffling from behind the door before it opened. Marcus opened the door with a 9 mm in his hand. "Damn, Amazon! You knocking like you crazy," he said as he tucked his 9 mm back in his waistband.

Immediately Amazon cocked back and swung with all his might, punching Marcus in his face, knocking him out instantly.

Kendu quickly rushed inside the apartment with his .45 drawn. "Don't fuckin' move!" He yelled, keeping Marcus's girl and some other grimy-looking guy in check.

"What's this all about, Amazon?" the grimy-looking man asked.

Amazon replied by smacking the shit outta him. "Did I say you could speak to me?" he growled. He pulled a knife from his back pocket. "Y'all niggas wanna steal money?" He flicked out the blade in a quick motion and started stabbing the man repeatedly until his body lay lifeless.

Amazon then turned to Marcus's girlfriend and grabbed a handful of her hair. "Get over here, bitch!" he yelled and plunged the knife in and out of the woman's chest.

Kendu looked on in amazement as Amazon put in that work.

Once Amazon finished with the woman, he turned his attention to Marcus, who was just now coming back around. He walked over and removed Marcus's 9 mm from his waist. "Get yo' bitch ass up!" He snatched him up by his neck and dragged him outside to the elevator.

Kendu just looked on and followed Amazon's lead.

When the elevator finally arrived, Amazon shoved Marcus inside and pressed the button for the top floor.

"Why you doing this for?" Marcus mumbled, holding his fractured jaw.

Once the elevator reached the top floor, Amazon shoved him out of the elevator and into the staircase.

"What the fuck you doing?" Marcus said with fear in his voice, as Amazon escorted him up to the roof.

"I'ma show you what we do to niggas with sticky fingers." Amazon lifted Marcus up over his head and walked over towards the edge of the roof.

Kendu watched on in disbelief. Just as he was about to say something, Amazon tossed Marcus off the roof.

Kendu quickly ran over to the ledge of the roof and looked down and saw Marcus sprawled out on top of a parked car. "You have a serious problem." Kendu shook his head, not believing what he just saw. "You need help."

"Had to make an example out of that clown before other niggas out in the streets think it's okay to start stealing money," Amazon said.

"I understand sending a message, but you be going overboard."

"Overboard?" Amazon echoed. "Today was a light day." He bust out laughing.

Diamond sat in Perry's office in the club, with her feet up, sipping on some coconut Cîroc. Ever since she had hooked up with Perry, life was sweet. Perry made sure she never wanted for anything and treated her like a queen. Sometimes Diamond found herself still thinking about Kendu, but she'd quickly erase him from her mind. He was now her past, and Perry was her future. Anything she wanted, all she had to do was ask. And Perry came straight home every night, so she never had to wonder or guess what he was out doing.

As Diamond sat chilling, she heard a light knock on the door before it opened.

"Hey, baby, you all right?" Perry said, peeking his head inside.

"Yes, baby. I'm fine." Diamond smiled. "What you doing? Checking up on me?"

"You know I'm going to always check up on you, baby." Perry came inside and planted a kiss on Diamond's lips. He sat on the edge of the desk.

"I'm a big girl that knows how to handle herself," she said in her sexy voice.

"Tell you what"—Perry leaned over and kissed on Diamond's neck. "Why don't you go to the house and wait for me to get there?" He handed her the keys to his BMW.

"You sure that's what you want?" Diamond asked in a seductive tone. She kissed him. "Sure you don't need me to help out around here?" she asked. But really she didn't feel like doing shit. All she wanted to do was go home and relax in the hot tub.

"You just make sure you ready for me when I get there." Perry smacked Diamond's ass as she left his office.

As Diamond made her way down the stairs, with each step she took, she could feel all eyes on her, all the jealous stares. It didn't matter to her, though. She held her head up high as she exited the club.

She hopped in Perry's BMW and peeled out the parking lot like she was on a high-speed chase.

Kendu stood on the block with Dirty Black and the rest of his crew just chilling. He was on his fourth drink, trying to drink away his problems, when he noticed an unfamiliar car pull up. Immediately his hand slid down to his waist, until he saw the driver get out the car and head his way. Spider walked with a cool bop until he reached Kendu.

"Yo', where the fuck you been at?" Kendu huffed. "I been calling you all week!"

"Yo', niggas ran up in the spot and tried to rob us," Spider told him. "I laid one nigga down and got up outta there."

"So why the fuck you ain't been answering when I called?"

"Because I'm wanted for murder!" Spider answered. "My moms called me, talking about they had kicked down her door looking for me, so I tossed my phone."

"How they know it was you?" Kendu asked, a puzzled look on his face.

"Somebody in our circle must of set it up 'cause I don't see how else niggas would connect that murder to me."

"You think that nigga Deuce had something to do with it?" Kendu asked.

"Not sure, but that nigga been acting kind of weird lately."

"Yo', what's good? Everything all right over here?" Dirty Black asked as he walked over.

"Yeah, everything cool," Kendu replied.

"A'ight. I'm just making sure." Dirty Black looked Spider up and down like he was a chump.

Before either man could say another word, a black minivan made a sharp stop across the street from the group of men.

"Yo', watch out. It's a hit!" Dirty Black yelled as he pulled his 9 mm from his waistband.

Kendu reached for his gun, but before he could reach it, he saw the minivan door slide open, and three machine guns come out firing.

Once the gunshots started banging out, everybody immediately got low. Before Spider had a chance to do anything, seven bullets ripped through his body, killing him instantly. After about a hundred rounds were fired, the minivan quickly sped off, burning rubber in the process.

Dirty Black quickly hopped up off the ground and chased the minivan halfway down the street, popping shots at the van.

Kendu went over and kneeled down by Spider's side. "Fuck!" he cursed loudly.

"Yo', come on. You can't stay here!" Dirty Black said as he grabbed Kendu up. "That nigga dead. Let's get the fuck up outta here." He slid in Amazon's truck and peeled off.

"Fuck!" Kendu cursed as he jogged across the street and jumped in his Acura and put the pedal to the metal.

Diamond pulled Perry's BMW into the gas station and pulled up right beside one of the pumps when she saw Kendu's Acura pull into the gas station.

"I know that's not him," she told herself as she slowly slid out the BMW.

Kendu pulled up to the pump right across from the BMW and hopped out the car, an angry look on his face and blood on his shirt. As he walked towards the front door of the gas station, he stopped and did a double-take when he saw Diamond. "Fuck you doing out here around this way?"

"Minding my business," Diamond said with much attitude.

"Oh, so it's like that?" Kendu nodded toward the BMW.

Diamond just waved him off as she began pumping her gas.

"You don't hear me talking to you?" Kendu growled. He grabbed Diamond and hemmed her up against the car. "How you just going to do this to me over some other nigga that you just met?"

"Perry knows how to treat a lady, unlike you." She looked at Kendu's hands on her shirt.

"You don't know nothing about that nigga." Kendu let go of Diamond's shirt. "For all you know, he could be a rapist or some shit."

"No. Perry is a gentleman, not an animal," she said, letting the last word roll off her tongue, as she motioned her head at the blood on his shirt.

"Oh, so now I'm an animal?" Kendu said, looking in her eyes. "I'm your husband, but yet you treating me like some clown out in the streets."

"Long story short," Diamond said, looking at the ground. "It's over. I don't want to be with you no more. I'm with Perry now. So I guess now you and your girlfriend Carmen can go live happily ever after."

"That's how you feel?" Kendu asked, not believing what he was hearing.

"That's exactly how I feel." Diamond hopped in the front seat of the BMW and stormed out of the gas station, leaving Kendu standing there.

Kendu stood in the gas station in a stupor. Him and Diamond had been married for five years, and of course, they had their share of problems, but it wasn't that bad to where he thought Diamond would ever leave him.

"What a muthafuckin' day!" Kendu smirked as he hopped in his Acura and headed home.

"I know I hit at least three of them clowns," Mousey boasted from the passenger seat of the minivan. "I'm tired of these clowns walking around like they untouchable and shit."

Deuce just drove in silence with a nervous look on his face. He kept a close eye on the other young goon who sat in the back of the van, through the rearview mirror. All Deuce wanted to do was get paid. All this unnecessary drama and gunplay wasn't in his plans, but in order to get that money, there wasn't much he wouldn't do.

"So what's next?"

"Fuck you mean, what's next?" Mousey looked at him like he was insane. "We already got a trap house set up a block away from Kendu's spot. Now that nigga Dirty Black is next."

"Dirty Black?" Deuce echoed. "Nah, now you biting off a little more than you can chew."

"You scared?" Mousey smirked at Deuce. He could see the fear in his eyes.

"Nah, I just like my life," Deuce replied, keeping his eyes on the road while he spoke.

"You let me worry about Dirty Black. Plus, I got a little surprise for him." Mousey had a devilish smirk on his face as he rubbed his hands together.

Diamond drove back to Perry's house in complete silence. All she could think about was Kendu. Of course she still loved him, but she just couldn't deal with his lying to her about Carmen and all his other women anymore. As much as she tried to push Kendu out of her mind, it was no use. He held a special place in her heart.

"Fuck him!" Diamond said out loud as she pulled up in Perry's driveway and let the engine die.

As she stepped inside Perry's crib, she immediately began to think about how good Perry treated her, compared to Kendu. She loved that, whatever she wanted, Perry would make sure she had it, no questions asked. She walked over to the fridge and poured herself a glass of wine as she headed upstairs so she could hop in the hot tub.

Before Diamond got in the hot tub, she decided she was going to be nosy and look all around Perry's crib. She kicked off her shoes and let her feet sink into the plush carpet as she walked through the house. She went from room to room looking inside closets, drawers, and everything. She thought there was something he wasn't telling her, so she searched his crib in hope of finding a woman's clothes and jewelry laying around.

After about twenty minutes of searching, Diamond came up empty. "Damn! Well, I guess this nigga is keeping it real with me," she said to herself as she looked straight ahead and saw the basement door. Immediately, she remembered that she had never been down there. Her curiosity quickly got the better of her.

She slowly walked over to the basement and turned the doorknob. "Fuck!" She cursed loudly when she realized the door was locked. "It must still be flooded down there." She shrugged her shoulders and went upstairs so she could relax in the hot tub.

Diamond stepped out the hot tub with a towel wrapped around her breasts and entered the bedroom. She stopped in mid-stride and grabbed her chest and took a deep breath.

"Damn! You scared the shit outta me," she said, looking at Perry, who sat on the bed with a bottle of red wine in his hand.

"I'm sorry, baby." Perry turned up the bottle and took a deep sip. "I knew you was in the hot tub. I didn't want to bother you," he said as he stood.

"Well, you got here just in time," Diamond said in a sexually charged voice. She let her towel drop to the floor.

Perry licked his lips and took another sip of the wine as he watched Diamond approach him. Diamond didn't speak, she just walked up to him, slid down to her knees and began to undo his belt buckle.

"What you doing, baby?" Perry asked with a smirk on his face as he felt his nature begin to rise.

"Shut the fuck up!" Diamond growled in her sexy voice. She began licking the tip of Perry's dick, working her tongue like a rattlesnake. "You like that, baby?"

Before Perry could reply, she took him all the way in her mouth as she tightly gripped the base of his dick and began jerking it, while the head of his dick rested in her mouth.

"Ohhhhh shit!" Perry moaned as he looked down and watched Diamond handle her business. He loved how she sucked, slobbed, and slurped all over his dick. "You love your dick?" he asked.

"Mmm-hmmm." Diamond continued to suck the shit out of his dick, never missing a beat.

"Your dick taste good?"

"Mmm-hmm."

Perry took another swig from his bottle of red wine, before he poured some on his dick. He watched as Diamond slurped it all off, trying not to let a drop hit the floor.

"Look at me, baby!" Perry grabbed a handful of Diamond's hair and began to fuck her mouth like never before.

Diamond moaned loudly, looking up at Perry the whole time as he fucked her mouth like it was a pussy. Perry aggressively stroked her mouth until he finally exploded in it. "Awwwwww!!" he groaned as his come shot out.

Diamond sucked out every last drop before swallowing it like it was nothing.

"Damn! That was the best head I ever got in whole life," Perry said, breathing heavily.

"It's plenty more where that came from." Diamond winked as she picked up the bottle of wine and took a deep swig.

"Can I ask you a question?" Perry asked, laying back on the bed with his eyes closed.

Diamond took another sip. "Yeah. What's up?"

"How long you going to keep wearing that wedding ring?"

"Damn! My bad. I didn't even know I still had it on. I've never taken off my ring, so I guess it was just kind of a habit," she said, struggling to get the ring off her finger. After about the fourth try, the ring finally slipped off. "Is that better?"

"Much better." Perry smiled as he leaned over and kissed Diamond on her lips.

"I'm going to ask you one more time." Dirty Black punched the Spanish man named Hector in his face again. "Who was that who shot at me the other night?"

"I swear to God, I don't know," Hector pleaded, scared for his life. "I got shot at too. I was with y'all, remember?" He looked around the room at the sea of angry black faces.

"We was on your block, so that makes you responsible." Dirty Black grabbed the .357 that one of his goons handed him. "Last chance."

"I swear on my grandmother's grave, I don't—"

Before he could finish his sentence, Dirty Black pulled the trigger, popping Hector's top like a Heineken. "Lyin' muthafucka! I want y'all niggas to get to the bottom of this for me.Whoever pulled that trigger, I want him or them brought to me ASAP!" He handed the dirty gun to Amazon, as the whole crew exited the small Bronx apartment.

Dirty Black stepped out the apartment building with an angry look on his face. He still couldn't believe somebody had the audacity to try to kill him. As him and his crew headed to their vehicles, he heard somebody calling his name. He looked over and saw Mousey leaning up against a silver Benz alongside two of his goons.

"Fuck you want, li'l nigga? I'm busy right now," Dirty Black said, not even giving Mousey enough respect to stop while he spoke.

"Yo', I said I need to talk to you, son!" Mousey said louder than he needed to, to get the point across that he wasn't playing.

Immediately Amazon, Kendu, and the rest of the crew looked at Mousey like he was crazy.

Amazon huffed. "Fuck you just said, li'l nigga?" as he headed over in Mousey's direction.

Dirty Black stopped him. He walked over to Mousey with a smirk on his face. "Fuck you want?"

"I need you to front me a hundred grams. I'm fucked up right now," Mousey said seriously.

"Nigga, you called me over here to ask me that?" Dirty Black said, ready to smack the shit outta the clown who stood in front of him.

"Oh, you too good to look out for a old friend now? You suppose to take care of the hood. What happen to looking out for your own peoples?"

"Nigga, you ain't my peoples. The only reason I ain't split your wig yet is because I used to run with your uncle Big Time back in the day before he got locked up."

"If I go back and tell him this, I don't think he would appreciate it," Mousey said with a little smirk on his face. He knew that his uncle Big Time would be getting released from prison in two weeks, that's why he was talking slick.

"Tell him what you want." Dirty Black was clearly getting upset. "I don't give a fuck!"

"A'ight, I'ma see you around," Mousey said, looking Dirty Black up and down.

Before Mousey could even turn to walk away, he felt a punch to the side of his head. He struggled to stay on his feet as he leaned up against his car for support.

Amazon and Kendu quickly pulled out their guns, just in case any of Mousey's goons were feeling a little froggy.

Everyone just looked on as Dirty Black beat the shit out of Mousey like he was a child. "Watch your fuckin' mouth when you talk to me!" Dirty Black snarled as he gave Mousey one last kick to his face before walking off, leaving him laid out in the middle of the street in a puddle of his own blood.

"These young niggas is outta control!" Dirty Black huffed from the passenger seat.

The truth of the matter was, Dirty Black never liked Mousey. He'd just been ignoring him out of respect for his uncle, but Mousey had crossed the line and had to get dealt with.

"Fuck that clown," Amazon said from behind the wheel. "I don't know why you ain't let me clap that nigga."

"Bigger fish to fry right now," Dirty Black reminded him. "I still need y'all to hit the street and find out who tried to kill me."

As Dirty Black and Amazon sat up front talking over their problems, Kendu sat in the back of the truck in deep thought. Half of his mind was on Diamond and what she was doing that very moment, while the other half of his mind was on Deuce and his whereabouts.

As Amazon drove, Kendu noticed they were cruising right by Deuce's crib. "Yo', pull over real quick," Kendu said.

"Why?" Amazon questioned, peeking at him through the rearview mirror.

"I gotta take care of something real quick."

Dirty Black signaled Amazon to pull over with a head nod, and the big man did as he was told. Kendu slid from the backseat and walked up to the passenger window. "I'ma swing by the spot later on, a'ight."

"Say no more." Dirty Black gave Kendu dap then the dark tinted window rolled up.

Kendu walked down the block towards Deuce's crib. If something was up with Deuce, he planned on finding out. As soon as he walked up on Deuce's apartment, he could hear Cam'ron and Vado's new mixtape blasting from inside the crib.

Knock! Knock! Knock!

As Kendu waited for someone to answer the door, he quickly checked his cell phone, making sure he had service and hadn't missed a call from Diamond.

Seconds later, a man wearing no shirt answered the door. "What's up?"

"Where Deuce at?" Looking past the man inside the apartment, Kendu could see about six other men.

"He busy right now."

"No Shirt" went to close the door, but Kendu quickly stuck his Nike boot in the door. "I need to talk to him now!"

No Shirt could see in Kendu's eyes that he wasn't playing and meant business. "A'ight, hold on." He stepped to the side so Kendu could enter. "Wait right here. I'll go get him." No shirt disappeared in the back.

Immediately Kendu got weird and angry stares from the other men in the apartment. His hand quickly rested on his waistline, where he gripped his .45 as he continued to wait.

Seconds later Deuce appeared from the back room. "What's good, my nigga?" he said, holding out his hand for dap.

"Fuck you got going on up here?" Kendu asked, leaving Deuce hanging.

"You been acting funny lately, so I opened up shop with the 'piff,'" Deuce said nonchalantly.

"So you opened up shop on your own without hollering at me or nothing?" Kendu asked. "I thought we was a team?"

Deuce looked him up and down. "We ain't been a team ever since you started fuckin' with that clown, Dirty Black."

"And you know exactly why I'm dealing with him in the first place," Kendu reminded him.

"A'ight. Just like you gotta do what you gotta do, so do I." Deuce scowled. "You not the only one with ideas."

Kendu couldn't believe what he was hearing. "Word? It's like that?"

"Just like that."

A smirk danced on Kendu's lip as he stared at Deuce for about ten seconds. Then he turned and headed out the door. A thousand thoughts ran through Kendu's mind. He couldn't understand Deuce's change of heart. "Fuck it! If he wanna do his own thing, then fuck it!" Kendu said to himself as he flagged down a cab.

Kendu sat in the back of the cab just reflecting on everything that had happened to him in the past couple of months.

***

Kendu paid the cab driver and slowly walked inside his empty house. Ever since Diamond had left, he just felt so alone and lost in the brain. As he stepped inside his empty house, he immediately missed his wife's presence. He walked over to the fridge, grabbed himself a bottle of wine and popped it open. Then he pulled out his cell phone and dialed Diamond's number.

Diamond checked herself out in the mirror one last time before heading out the door. Since she was now Perry's girl, she no longer had to work at the club, but she would still go anyways some nights, just to help out. She stepped out the house and slid in her new all-white Audi A8. She pulled out into the streets like she owned them. She was speeding to the club so she could see Perry, when she heard her phone ringing. She looked at the caller ID, sucked her teeth, then answered. "What do you want?"

"Can I please talk to you?" Kendu asked desperately.

"Nah, I really ain't got nothing to say to you, Kendu."

"I can't just let you go like that. Please just meet me for dinner or something, so we can talk."

"I'll think about it," Diamond replied nonchalantly.

"Well, think hard and call me back if you want to meet up."

"Yeah."

Diamond pulled up into the club's parking lot and quickly pulled into the VIP parking spot. She stepped out her ride, and all eyes were on her. She made sure she threw a little extra in her walk as her heels stabbed the concrete.

"Hey, Shawn. What's up?" she asked, walking up to the bouncer, who guarded the front door with his life.

"Hey, Diamond. How you feeling tonight?" Shawn asked, his arms open for a hug.

"I'm good." She gave him a friendly-pat-on-the-back hug. "How it's looking in there?" she asked as she passed the huge man.

"Oh, it's poppin'!" Shawn yelled over his shoulder, a smirk on his face.

Diamond stepped foot in the club, and immediately the bass from the speaker and the heat slapped her in the face. Young Jeezy's song, "Lose My Mind," was blaring through the speakers and had the club jumping. As she snaked her way through the crowd, she felt someone grab her wrist and looked up to see a handsome gentleman standing in front of her.

Diamond took her hand back. "Can I help you?"

"You can start by telling me your name."

"My name?" Diamond echoed. "First of all, who are you?"

"Everyone calls me Rock," he said, looking down at his crotch.

"Rock, huh?" Diamond replied with a smirk. "Sorry, Rock," she said, letting his name roll off her tongue. "But I already have a man. A real one at that."

"What's his name?"

"Why?"

"Because I know everybody, and I can tell you right now what the nigga is about and if he's official or not."

"His name is Perry," Diamond said proudly.

"Serial killer Perry?" Rock broke out into a laughing fit. "Girl, you better leave that nigga alone before you end up tied up in his basement like the rest of his girls."

"Huh?" Diamond asked, a confused look on her face. "What are you talking about?"

Before Rock could reply, Perry cut in. "What's going on over here?" His voice was calm, but Rock got the message loud and clear.

"What?" Rock shrugged his shoulders. "We was just talking."

"Listen, my man," Perry said, leaning in closer so Rock could hear him clearly, "go talk to somebody else."

Rock's eyes went from Perry to Diamond then back to Perry. "You got it, bossman," he said as he backed away and blended into the crowd.

"Why was you over here entertaining that clown?" Perry asked in a calm voice.

"I wasn't. As I was walking through, he grabbed my arm."

"Do me a favor." Perry bent down and hugged Diamond. "Go home and wait for me to get there."

Diamond thought about protesting 'cause she had just got there, but quickly decided against it. "Okay, baby. Are you all right?"

"Yes, baby. I'm fine. Just got a few things I have to take care of," he told her as he gave her a kiss.

"Okay, baby. Don't work too hard." Diamond turned and headed towards the club's exit.

Diamond slid behind the wheel of her new car, and didn't feel like going straight home, especially since she was all dressed up, and the night was just beginning. She pulled out her cell phone and dialed Kendu's number.

On the fourth ring he finally answered. "Yo."

"You still wanna go out and talk?" she asked.

"Yeah. Meet me at your favorite restaurant in thirty minutes," Kendu told her.

"A'ight. On my way."

Diamond pulled out the parking lot like she was a professional racecar driver. For the entire ride her mind went back to what Rock had told her inside the club. "Why would he say something like that about Perry?" she thought out loud.

***

Diamond pulled up in front of her favorite soul food restaurant and saw Kendu standing out front. She was thankful there was a parking spot right in front of the restaurant. She looked in the rearview mirror just to make sure her makeup and lip gloss was on point. She slid out the Audi with a serious look on her face.

Kendu opened his arms for a hug. "Hey, baby."

"Wassup," Diamond replied in a dry tone. She gave him the friendly hug with the pat on the back.

The two walked in the restaurant and were quickly seated at a booth by the window.

"So what's up?" Diamond said as she browsed through the menu, even though she already knew what she wanted.

"What you mean, what's up? I want you to come home where you belong."

"You got too much going on right now for me," Diamond said, waving him off. "Shit, I'm ready for, you're not."

"But that clown at the club is, though, right?"

"Perry knows how to treat a lady," Diamond said in a matter-of-fact tone. "Plus, even if he doesn't have time for me, he makes time—something you know nothing about."

"Listen—"

"Are y'all ready to order?" the scrawny white man asked politely, with his pen and notepad in his hand.

After the two ordered what they wanted, Kendu continued his rant. "I am your husband, and you told me 'til death do us part."

"Well, you should've thought about that before you went out giving away my dick like it was free lunch." Diamond's voice cracked a little bit.

"What is you talking about?" Kendu said, faking ignorance. "All I was trying to do was get this money so Dirty Black and his army didn't kill me, but now I got that all worked out and I want you home!"

"I have a new home now."

Kendu slammed his fist down on the table, getting scared and strange stares from the other diners in the restaurant. "Fuck that nigga Perry! You don't even know shit about him!"

Immediately Diamond's mind went back to what Rock had just told her in the club.

"Look, I am a grown woman. And if I want to be with Perry, then that's my choice. Just like you chose to go fuck with that bitch Carmen." She said it like she had just said something powerful.

"Is that what this is about? Payback?" Kendu asked, a disgusted look on his face. "Okay, you got me back, and now it's time for you to come home."

Just as Diamond was about to respond, her phone rang. Immediately her eyes looked up at Kendu like she had been busted, but then she quickly remembered their current situation. She looked at her phone and saw Perry's name flashing across the screen. She let it ring out before she continued what she had to say.

"I just think it's best if we do our own thing."

"Why you didn't answer the phone for your boyfriend?" Kendu smirked.

She quickly shot back, "He don't own me!"

"When are you coming back home, baby? I miss you." Kendu pleaded, as he held her hands in his.

"I can't do that right now," Diamond said, not able to look Kendu in his eyes when she answered him.

"I understand." Kendu released her hands as he stood up. He looked at her one last time before he dropped a few twenties on the table, turned, and made his way towards the exit.

Diamond just sat there and watched as Kendu exited the restaurant. Inside she wanted to die, but she knew she had to remain strong, 'cause Kendu had his chance and he blew it, and now it was Perry's turn. She sat in the restaurant for about twenty more minutes before she got up and headed home.

Rock stumbled out the club. He tried to lean on a bouncer to regain his balance but quickly got pushed down to the ground. "Punk-ass bitch!" he yelled as he struggled back up to his feet and continued on through the parking lot.

Perry snaked his way through the parking lot like a ninja as he slid his fingers inside his black leather gloves. He saw Rock stumbling through the parking lot and knew, if he was going to make a move, it would have to be now. He pulled a sharp hunting knife from the small of his back as he crept up on Rock from behind.

Once he got close enough he quickly covered Rock's mouth with a gloved hand and smoothly slit his throat with the other hand. He watched as Rock dropped to the ground, struggling not to choke on his own blood.

"Learn how to mind your business next time!" Perry huffed as he jabbed the knife repeatedly in and out of Rock's chest and stomach until he was sure the man was dead. "Clown!" He growled as he stomped Rock's head into the ground before he smoothly walked off, and blended into the night like ain't nothing even happen.

For the entire ride home Kendu listened to Drake's song, "Find Your Love," as he weaved in and out of the highway lanes. He just couldn't understand why Diamond was making this so difficult for him. There was no way she was in love with that clown from the club that fast. For a second he thought about going up to the club and catching a charge, but then he decided against it and just went home instead. Perry had won fair and square, and there was nothing he could do about it but move on.

Chapter 10

Diamond slid out of her Audi and quickly strolled towards the front door, tired and in desperate need of a shower. She stepped inside the house and closed and locked the door. Just as she turned around, Perry grabbed her by her shirt and violently shoved her back up against the door. "Where the fuck you been at?" he growled with a murderous look in his eyes.

"Ummm, I went to go get something to eat," she answered quickly.

"With who?" Perry questioned, never releasing his grip.

"By myself." She winced in pain. "Get the fuck off of me! You hurting me!"

Perry quickly released his grip and looked at her like she was insane. "Did you just curse at me?"

"Yeah!" Diamond yelled. "You was fuckin' hurting me," she said, fixing her shirt. "What the fuck! I just went to go get something to eat. What's the big fuckin' deal?"

"I don't know what kind of niggas you used to dealing with, but you about to fix this right now." Perry slowly took off his belt and let the buckle swing freely. "Now I gotta teach you some manners." He forcefully swung the belt, hitting Diamond on the shoulder and part of her neck.

Immediately Diamond dropped down to the floor and balled up as Perry struck her with the buckle of his belt at least thirty times before he headed upstairs, leaving her curled up in the corner with whelps and bruises all over her body.

Diamond lay on the floor crying her eyes out. She had never experienced that kind of pain in her life. Something inside of her wanted to leave and go back home, but her pride wouldn't let her, especially after how she had just shitted on Kendu at dinner. There was no way she could go back to him now.

She struggled to get back up to her feet and made her way to the downstairs bathroom so she could check out her wounds in the bathroom mirror.

Kendu found a parking spot in front of the park Dirty Black had told him to meet him at. When he got out the car, he saw the park was filled with women and guys, two speakers set up in the corner and the sound of Gucci Mane bumping through the speakers. He quickly spotted Dirty Black in the middle of the mix, showing off as usual.

"Fuck going on out here?" Kendu asked as he gave Dirty Black a pound.

"You know I love giving back to the hood." Dirty Black smiled. "Everybody know I throw the best cookouts in the city."

"It's mad hoes out here," Kendu said, checking out the few women standing around in tight booty shorts and heels.

"You already know how I do. Whenever you ready to get over your old lady, just let me know."

Kendu smirked. "Who on the grill? 'Cause that food is smelling mad good."

"Some fiend," Dirty Black said nonchalantly.

"Fuck you mean, some fiend?"

"Nah." Dirty Black laughed. "He a fiend now, but back in the day he used to be a chef. Trust me, that nigga be cooking his ass off."

Kendu was about to say he would never eat a fiend's cooking, but the food smelled too good for him to pass up on. He followed Dirty Black over to the table where Amazon and the rest of the crew sat getting their eat on.

As soon as he sat down, one of the girls wearing the booty shorts sat down next to him. "Hey, I'm Kiki."

"What's up?" Kendu said dryly.

"You mind if I sit here?" Kiki said, openly checking Kendu out.

"Yeah, you cool."

"Forgive him, Kiki," Dirty Black cut in from the sideline. "My man Kendu is a little shy, if you know what I mean."

"Oh really?" Kiki said with a smirk.

As if right on cue, Dem Franchize Boyz song, "White Tee," came blasting through the speakers, causing the crowd to erupt in a loud "Heeey!"

"This my muthafuckin' song," Kiki said out loud as she got up and began dancing like a stripper would, standing directly in front Kendu.

Kendu helped himself to a cup of Hennessy as he sat back and enjoyed the show. Kiki gyrated her hips like it was a slinky, as everyone looked on. She quickly turned around and bent over directly in front of Kendu's face and began making her ass clap. "You still shy?" she said, looking back at him, her ass clapping and jiggling.

Kendu just smiled and smacked her ass. His smile quickly faded away when he saw Mousey enter the park with a twenty-man entourage.

"Yo', ma, go get you and me something to drink real quick," Kendu said, dismissing Kiki before something popped off.

When Amazon noticed Mousey and his crew strolling through the park, he quickly grabbed his .45 that he had stashed in the garbage can and stood to his feet. Dirty Black's whole crew quickly formed behind him. Right before the two crews met head-on, a diesel nigga cut in front of Mousey and removed his shirt, showing off all his tattoos and big muscles.

"Y'all muthafuckas got a lot of nerves, crashing my cookout," Dirty Black said, taking in the whole crew.

"Crashing?" Big Time smiled. "We should've been invited in the first place."

Back in the day Big Time and his crew would've been invited, but Dirty Black knew the man standing in front of him wasn't the man he remembered. Jail had changed him and turned him into a more ruthless animal. Everybody had heard the stories about him putting in work behind the wall.

"When you get out?" Dirty Black asked.

"Two days ago." Big Time sized Dirty Black up, a tactic he had picked up in jail. "But fuck all that. My li'l nephew told me y'all got a problem."

"We ain't got no problem. Ya nephew was out of line, so I had to check him."

"He told me he just asked for a few things on consignment, and you shitted on him then sucker-punched him when he wasn't looking."

"Listen," Dirty Black said, getting annoyed, "I didn't like how the nigga came at me, so I washed him up."

Big Time smiled and looked in Dirty Black's eyes before he replied. "I'm willing to forget about all of this if you toss me a few of them thangs on the strength"—he paused—"you can call it a coming-home gift."

"Negative," Dirty Black said quickly. "Matter of fact, I'm tired of talking. You got thirty seconds to get the fuck up outta my park," he said as he coolly walked off.

Big Time was about to say something, but Amazon quickly jumped in his face. "Nineteen!" he counted through clenched teeth.

"I'ma have fun with you," Big Time said with a smile, as him and his team backed up out the park. Him and Amazon continued to eye-box until Big Time and his crew was finally out of the park.

Dirty Black sat over in the cut sipping on some coconut Cîroc. He knew Big Time was going to be a problem. A big one at that. Dirty Black kind of felt bad because, back in the day, he used to look up to Big Time, but now Big Time couldn't see himself looking up to a li'l nigga he used to son.

"Everything all right?" Kendu helped himself to a drink.

Dirty Black downed his drink in one gulp. "Yeah. Everything good."

"Who was that nigga?"

"Big Time." Dirty Black poured himself another drink. "He used to be a cool dude back in the day. Nigga had the whole hood scared of him."

"Damn! He get it in like that?" Kendu took a sip.

Dirty Black smirked. "Yeah, Big Time is certified, and I know jail only made him even worse."

"So why not just put him down on the team?"

"He the type that's used to being a boss," Dirty Black told him. "Working for me, it would only be a matter of time before he tried to take me out, and take over. I can't afford that right now."

Kendu could already see some shit about to pop off between the two. "That's crazy."

Dirty Black had no problem hitting Big Time off with some work and a couple of dollars as a coming-home gift, but he didn't like Big Time's approach. It kind of made him feel like he was trying to extort him. That's why he'd dismissed him so abruptly.

"Fuck that nigga!" Amazon cut in. "I hope he act up so I can light his ass up!" Back in the day, Big Time had murdered Amazon's father over thirty dollars.

Amazon sat in the living room playing Nintendo 64 as his father sat at the kitchen table getting high, the sound of Al Greene filling the apartment.

"Hey, boy!" Terry called out to his son. "Put that damn game down and come here!"

Amazon sucked his teeth as he paused his game and made his way over to the table. Every time his pops was high, he would always talk him to death and lecture him. "What?" he said with attitude.

"Fuck you mean, what?" Terry raised his hand and back-slapped Amazon across the face. "Get over here, that's what!"

Terry chopped up the small rock that sat in front of him with a twenty-five-cent razor. "I'm trying to teach you something, and you got the nerve to have an attitude," he continued to rant. "You see this?" he asked, looking up at his son.

"Yeah," Amazon answered with a frown on his face.

"What is it?" Terry quizzed him.

"Crack," Amazon replied.

"That's right." Terry placed a small pebble in his stem. "You better not ever let me catch you fuckin' with this shit, you hear me?" He grabbed Amazon by his collar.

"Yeah."

"Yeah, this shit ain't for you. I need you to promise me something." Terry took a quick hit right in front of his son.

Amazon looked away while his father took a long drag from the stem. "What?"

"Promise me you going to finish school and make it to the NFL, like we talked about." The corners of Terry's mouth started to slightly foam. "Promise me right now!"

"I promise."

"Thank you." Terry took another hit in front of his son. "Okay, you can go back to playing your game," he said, exhaling the smoke through his nose.

Terry was about to say something else, but before he could even get the words out, somebody kicked his front door open. Four men quickly rushed the apartment and tackled him out of the chair he was sitting in. Seconds later Big Time strolled up in the apartment like he owned it.

"Big Time, what's this all about?" Terry asked from the floor.

"You know exactly what the fuck this is about," Big Time said with a smile. "You snatched some work from one of my workers and ran."

"I had twenty-six dollars and he wouldn't let me go for three," Terry said, pleading his case. "He was a new jack, so I know he didn't know I was a loyal customer. So I just took that shit," he said nonchalantly. "You know I'ma get that back to you."

"You know my number one rule, Terry," Big Time said, pulling a .38 from the small of his back. "No stealing," he reminded him. "If it's one thing I hate, it's a thief."

"Come on, man. Please don't do this," Terry begged in front of his son.

"Are you begging, muthafucka?" Big Time hurried over to Terry and stomped him in his face. "You wasn't begging when you stole my shit!"

"I'm sorry. Please don't do this," Terry continued to beg.

"Stand that nigga up," Big Time ordered, his pistol aimed at Terry's chest.

"Noooooo!" Amazon yelled, charging toward the man holding the gun.

Big Time quickly side-stepped the big kid and hit him on top of his head with the gun, dropping him instantly. He then turned his attention back to Terry. "Hold that nigga up!"

"Wait please!" Terry begged. "Not in front of my son, please."

Big Time paused for a second. "Take this mutha-fucka outside."

One of Big Time's goons stood over Amazon, making sure he didn't move, while Big Time and his crew roughly escorted Terry outside.

Amazon lay on the floor crying not because he was hurt, but because he couldn't help his father. All he could hear was loud bumps and banging against the wall, followed by a slap, then his father begging again. Not too long after, he heard thirteen shots go off, one after another, followed by silence. Right then and there he knew his father had just been killed.

"Don't worry about that clown. If he act up, we gon' lay his ass down point-blank," Dirty Black said, snapping Amazon out of his trance.

Amazon still felt a certain way about what happened to his father. "I think we should go at that clown *before* he decides to bring it to us."

"We getting money," Dirty Black reminded him. "We can't be sitting around worrying about these broke niggas."

"You right," Amazon said, but deep down he was ready to go put in some work.

"I'm about to get up outta here." Kendu gave Dirty Black and Amazon both a pound. "Y'all need me to do anything tonight?"

Dirty Black told him, "Nah, you got the night off, champ."

"A'ight. If y'all need me, just holla," Kendu said as he walked off.

When Kendu reached his car, he no longer wanted to go home. He was tired of just sitting in the house all alone by himself. He didn't feel like hanging out at Carmen's crib either. "Fuck it," he said to himself as he slid in his car and headed to the nearest bar.

From the outside Kendu could see the lounge was crowded. He slid his .45 under his seat as he got out of his whip and headed toward the entrance. After waiting on line for ten minutes he was finally searched and allowed to enter the lounge. The packed lounge had a cool setup. Immediately, he made his way over to the bar and helped himself to a seat on an empty stool.

"What can I get you?" the bartender asked in a friendly tone.

"Vodka and orange juice."

Kendu scanned the entire place while the bartender prepared his drink. Seconds later the bartender handed him his drink. "Thanks." He took a sip.

No matter how hard Kendu tried not to think about Diamond, he just couldn't help himself. She just stayed on his mind. He wanted to know where she was, what she was doing, and who she was doing it with.

As he sat at the bar sipping on his drink, he heard a few other guys say, "Daaamn!" as all their eyes headed toward the entrance. Kendu turned to see what had

the men acting like zombies. He saw a beautiful light-
skinned woman walk up in the lounge like she owned
the place, her heels stabbing the floor with each step
she took. Just by looking at her face, you could tell that
she knew she was the shit.

"Damn!" Kendu mumbled. The woman's ass was so
big, he could see it from the front.

The woman came and sat on the empty stool right
next to him. "Hey, Henry," she said, calling the bartender by his name.

"Hey, Crystal. Haven't seen you in a while. Where
have you been?" Henry said, as if he was happy to see
her. Actually he was, 'cause Crystal was a good tipper.

"It's a long story, Henry." Crystal fanned herself with
her hand. "Let me get a bottle of vodka. It doesn't matter what kind, and I need some cranberry juice to go
with that."

When Henry returned with Crystal's bottle of Cîroc
and cranberry juice, Kendu quickly told him, "Let me
get another vodka and orange juice."

Crystal looked over at him like he was crazy. "You
don't see this big-ass bottle of Cîroc sitting right here?"

"Yeah. But you look like you about to punish that,"
Kendu joked.

"How about we punish it together?"

"I'm down," he said smoothly.

"Henry, let me get some orange juice over here,"
Crystal said as she started on her first drink.

Once Kendu had his orange juice, he poured himself
another drink and scooted his stool closer to Crystal.
"So where you from and all that?"

"I'm from Miami, but I been living in New York for
about twelve years now."

"Damn. What brought you all the way from Miami to
the city that never sleeps?"

"A man, of course."

"It's all good." Kendu noticed the embarassed look on her face. "Love done made everybody do some crazy things."

"I thought he was the one. But, come to find out, he wasn't."

"What happened, if you don't mind me asking?"

"Turns out that muthafucka was crazy!" Crystal said, shaking her head. "He was so nice in the beginning. Then, after a year or two, things just changed."

"I can dig it." Kendu took a sip from his glass. "Any kids?"

"Yes, I have a beautiful daughter," she said proudly. "So enough about me. You have any kids?"

"Not yet," Kendu replied with a smile.

"You want any?"

"Of course."

"You single?" Crystal helped herself to another drink.

"Yeah and no."

"Explain," Crystal said with a warm smile.

"Well, legally I'm married, but me and my wife are no longer together."

"Well, you wanna know what I think? I think it's her loss."

That last comment brought a smile to Kendu's face. Coming to the lounge turned out to be a good idea after all. "So are you single?"

"Yes, I am."

Kendu gave her a disbelieving look.

"What's that look for?"

"Just hard to believe that a woman as fine as yourself is single. I mean, I know men throw themselves at you all day every day."

"They do, but that doesn't mean I have to have a man. Actually this is my first time out in over eight months. And I only came here 'cause I didn't want to go to no club. Just needed to get out the house."

"That's the same way I was feeling tonight." Kendu smiled. "So are you looking for a new man?"

"No, not really." Crystal stirred her drink. "I'm about to move back to Miami at the end of the month."

"Damn! I just met you, and you ready to leave me already?"

"No. I love New York. But my crazy ex-boyfriend just got out of jail, and he's been sending me threatening letters before he got released, and I just don't got time for all that drama."

"Is that the guy you had your daughter with?"

"Yeah, but I don't want him around her with all that foolishness. He's ignorant and crazy."

"You never know. He might've changed his life around."

Crystal smirked. "Trust me, he's one that's never gonna change."

An hour later, and on their second bottle of Cîroc, Kendu and Crystal were still at the bar enjoying each other's company.

"You seem like a real cool guy," Crystal said, looking in Kendu's eyes.

"That's because I am."

Kendu returned her stare, and the two got caught up, staring in each other's eyes, until Crystal said, "Damn! This my shit!"

Kendu's face crumpled up when he heard "Teach Me How to Dougie" blasting through the speakers. "This your song?" He thought she was too old to like the song.

"Yes!"

Crystal grabbed Kendu's wrist and dragged him to the dance floor. As soon as the two hit the dance floor, she pressed her ass up against his dick and started seductively gyrating her hips to the beat, looking back at him the whole tine. Kendu flowed with the beat, matching her step for step. Just from dancing with her, Kendu could tell that her sex game was off the hook.

After the dance, the two made their way back over towards the bar.

"Yo', I had a blast, but I gotta get ready to get up outta here." Kendu downed what he had left in his glass in one gulp.

"You gotta leave right now?" Crystal asked, a disappointed look on her face.

"If I don't, I'm not going to be able to make it home," he replied honestly.

Crystal finished off her last glass. "I know you just met me and all that, but you wanna take this back to my place?"

"If you cool with that, I'm down."

"We just going to chill though, all right."

"Cool," Kendu said as the two stumbled out the lounge.

When the two got outside, they both agreed that neither one of them was in any condition to drive, so they walked over to the corner and flagged down a cab.

"What about our cars?" Crystal slurred.

"We'll just come back and get 'em tomorrow," Kendu replied as they slid in the back of the cab.

After a twenty-minute ride, the cab driver pulled up in front of Crystal's house. Kendu paid the cab driver then escorted her inside her own house. Once inside the house Kendu laid Crystal down on her couch. He could tell by how expensive the house looked that she couldn't have worked a regular job and been able to maintain it.

"Damn! This a nice-ass house. Can I move in?" Kendu joked.

Crystal chuckled with her eyes closed as she lay on the couch. "My ex I was telling you about was a big drug dealer before he went to jail."

"I see," Kendu said, looking around.

He went to say something else but stopped mid-sentence when he heard Crystal lightly snoring. He just smiled and removed her shoes for her. Then he found himself a nice spot on the floor and called it a night.

Chapter 11

The next morning Kendu woke up to the smell of turkey bacon and home fries. He got up from off the carpet and saw Crystal in the kitchen with some tight stretch pants and a wife-beater standing over the stove.

"Damn! You fine *and* you know how to cook." Kendu stretched.

"I do it all," Crystal said with a smile. "I hope you hungry."

"Starving."

"Okay, it will be ready in five minutes," she told him. "Oh, and there's a brand-new toothbrush in the bathroom with your name written on it." She laughed.

"Oh, you got jokes." Kendu laughed as he disappeared in the bathroom.

After Kendu came out the bathroom, him and Crystal enjoyed a nice turkey bacon, pancakes, and eggs breakfast that she prepared for them.

They laughed and joked all morning, getting to know one another, until Kendu received a text message from Dirty Black that read:

I need to holla at you, young'un. The sooner the better.

"I already know." Crystal said. "You gotta go, right?"

"Yeah, gotta go handle some business. If you ain't doing nothing later on, call me and we can hang out again."

Kendu decided to call a cab. Five minutes later he heard the cab driver outside beeping his horn.

"Yo', scream me later, and I'll swing back through to see you."

The two hugged and kissed each other on the cheek.

"I'ma call you later, okay," Crystal said as she watched him leave from the doorway. "Be careful."

Kendu yelled over his shoulder, "You already know," and slid in the back of the cab.

Crystal watched the cab pull off and bend the corner. Just as she was about to go back inside the house, she saw a Suburban on chrome rims pull up in her driveway.

"Who the fuck is this?" she thought out loud.

Big Time slid out of the Suburban with a cold-ice grill on his face. Crystal immediately closed the door and put the chain lock on the door. Seconds later she heard a hard knock at the door. *Bang! Bang! Bang!*

She opened up the door as far as the chain would allow. "What are you doing here?"

"So I ain't seen you in five years, and the first time I do, I see a nigga running up out ya crib," Big Time said, a smirk on his face.

"Me and you been over for years," Crystal told him. "And I have the right to see anybody I want to."

"So is that nigga the reason I haven't seen you in over five years and you haven't replied to any of my letters?" Big Time said, looking in Crystal's eyes. He knew back in the day he did her wrong, but now that he was out, he wanted to get back with her and show her things would be different this time around. But the look in her eyes told him that she wasn't having that.

"A man has nothing to do with anything. Me and you been over for years. You don't remember all the nights I cried and begged you to spend time with me? What about all the women? Yeah, you remember. Then you wonder why I ain't answer none of your letters." She shook her head in disgust. "You ain't got nobody to blame but yourself."

"I know I fucked up back in the day. But now I'm here to make things right. Give me a second chance."

"Sorry. You're all out of chances." Crystal knew Big Time did miss her, but she also knew he was the type of guy who couldn't change even if his life depended on it. "It's a million other women out there. Why don't you go and get one of them?"

"I don't want them, I want you. I need you. All I'm asking for is another chance. And what about my daughter?"

"What about her?" Crystal asked, looking at Big Time like he was insane.

"Fuck this shit! Open up this fuckin' door!"

Crystal quickly tried to shut the door and lock it, but Big Time kicked it open. "I'm tired of fuckin' playing with ya ass!" He grabbed Crystal and slammed her down on the couch. "You belong to me!" he growled, forcing his mouth on hers and sloppily kissing her. "I paid for this muthafuckin' house, and you gon' try and talk to me through the door?"

"Get off of me!" Crystal yelled as she tried her best to get him off her.

Big Time growled, "Listen, bitch, I'ma be back tomorrow." He grabbed a handful of her hair and forced her to look at him. "Make sure my daughter is here! We gon' be a family, whether you like it or not!" He let go of Crystal's hair then turned around and smacked the shit out of her. "Next time, watch your mouth when you talking to me. Daddy is back home." Big Time turned and exited the house.

Not knowing what to do, Crystal just lay on the floor and cried her eyes out. Not only was she scared of Big Time, but she also knew that, no matter where she went, he would eventually find her.

Chapter 12

Diamond stepped out the shower and dried herself off. She looked in the mirror and examined all the bruises on her body. She still couldn't believe that Perry had whipped her with a belt like she was an animal. At this point she didn't know what to do. She wanted to go back home, but after the way she had treated Kendu, she knew going home was no longer an option.

She stepped out the bathroom and saw flowers and balloons laid all over the room, a big teddy bear on the bed, and a note next to her pillow. She opened the note and began to read it:

"Baby, first of all I want to apologize for how I reacted the other night. I just be so afraid I'm going to lose you, and that I wouldn't know how to take it. You are the best thing to ever happen to me. Please forgive me. I had to run to the club real quick. I should be back in about an hour. I love you."

She crumpled up the note, and quickly looked at the clock on the wall. *Two-fifteen.* She had only been in the shower for about fifteen minutes, which meant she had about forty-five minutes before Perry returned. She quickly threw on some sweatpants and a wife-beater, and ran downstairs as fast as she could.

She made it to the living room and stared at the basement door. She couldn't help herself. She had to find out what was down there. Ever since Rock had mentioned something about being "tied up in Perry's basement like the rest of his women," she'd been wondering, and now was the perfect time to find out.

She walked over to the counter and grabbed the credit card that Perry left in case of an emergency. When see reached the basement door, she quickly slid the card in between the lock and managed to get the door open. Diamond was nervous about going down the basement steps. "Get it together," she told herself as she built up enough courage and began to head down the steps.

When she made it all the way down, she turned on the light and began to look around.

Instead of going to the club, Perry went to the bank so he could grab some cash real quick and take Diamond out to dinner, to make things right with her. Deep down inside he knew she was a good woman, but from his past he knew how sneaky women could be. So with that, he decided to keep Diamond on a short leash. Once Perry left the bank, he hopped in his car and headed straight back home.

Diamond walked around the basement looking around. She had been down there for about fifteen minutes, and she still hadn't found anything out of the ordinary. "Come on, I know it has got to be something down here," she said to herself out loud as she continued to search the basement.

She spotted a shovel over in the corner by the washer and dryer. Just as she was about to go over to investigate, she heard a car door slam. Immediately her heart dropped down to her stomach.

She ran and cut the light out and stormed up the basement steps. She ended up fumbling with the lock on the door, trying to leave the door the same way she'd found it. Once she heard the lock click, she quickly closed the basement door and walked over to the counter just as Perry was walking in the house.

"Hey, baby. What you doing down here?" Perry asked as he looked around.

"Nothing. I just came down here to get something to drink."

"You still mad at me, baby?" He removed some flowers from behind his back.

"No, baby. I'm not mad at you anymore," Diamond lied. "I was wrong. I should've went straight home like you asked me to."

"You forgive me, baby?" Perry leaned in and began to kiss and lick on her neck.

"Yes, baby," Diamond moaned. "Baby, did you ever get that flood fixed down in the basement?"

Perry effortlessly lifted Diamond up and sat her on top of the counter. "No, not yet, baby. You missed me while I was gone?" He slid down her sweatpants.

Diamond nodded her head yes as she watched Perry go down and spread her legs all the way open.

"Damn! I missed you," he said, talking to her pussy. He opened up her lips with his thumbs and dove in face first.

Diamond threw her head back in pleasure as she held on tightly to the back of his head. Perry sucked and licked all over Diamond's pussy until she finally released in his mouth. He then picked her up off the counter and carried her upstairs, where the two had the best makeup sex ever.

Chapter 13

Big Time pulled up in front of the house him and his crew hung out at. Today was a special day. It was the first day of the takeover. Big Time had called a meeting and planned on revealing his plan to his new team. Soon as he pulled up, one of his six-foot-four goons stood at the curb with a gun visibly in his waistband. He opened up the door for him then escorted him inside the house.

Big Time stepped foot inside the house and saw that all his soldiers were there on time, and was ready for the takeover. "Listen up!" he announced, getting everyone's attention. "First of all, let me say, if anybody is scared, get the fuck out now!" When nobody got up to leave, he continued, "this clown Dirty Black been on top while I was away, but now it's time for me and my team to get back to where we belong."

All his goons cheered.

He silenced them with a raise of his hand. "Yo', Action Jackson, come up here for a second."

Everybody looked on as a slim, light-skinned cat with deep waves in his hair walked up and stood next to Big Time.

"Everybody, this right here is my man Action Jackson." Big Time said, introducing him to the rest of the crew. "I was locked up with this guy, and all I can say is, I finally think I met somebody who's crazier than me." Big Time laughed. "Me and him are going to be in charge of laying down the law out here in these streets."

He paused. "Mousey and Deuce, y'all in charge of making sure the product is getting moved and the money is being collected. The only way we going to take over is by working as a team."

"How we going to take over?" a younger soldier asked. "I mean, Dirty Black and his team is deep out here in these streets."

Big Time chuckled before he answered that question. "Territory," he said. "We going to take over blocks and set up trap houses all over. If we want something, we going to have to take it. Right now we have four trap houses popping. By the end of the month, I want to have ten. This meeting is over. Let's go make this shit happen."

Big Time sat down as he watched all his soldiers exit the house. He poured himself a shot of Grey Goose as he mentally prepared himself for what was about to go down. While he was locked up, he had heard stories about how ruthless Dirty Black and his crew was, and how everyone that went up against him had failed miserably. Big Time was an O.G., and he wasn't scared to get his hands dirty. His motto was, it's either going to be us, or it's going to be them.

He downed another shot as Action Jackson came and sat down next to him.

"Who we hitting first?" Action Jackson asked, getting straight to the point. He had a low tolerance for nonsense, and he could sit still but for so long. Talking only made him angrier. That's how he got the name *Action*.

"First, we going to send a few messages to the streets to let muthafuckas know we ain't playing," Big Time informed him.

"I'm ready right now," Action Jackson said, slipping his fingers in his black leather gloves.

Big Time and Action Jackson got up and headed for the door. Big Time looked over his shoulder and yelled, "I'll be back in a few. Y'all niggas get this money." Then him and Action Jackson disappeared out the front door.

Perry sat in his office at the club in deep thought. The past few weeks with Diamond had been wonderful, but there were the little things that she did that made him second-guess if she was the one or not, or even if she was worthy of keeping her life. As he sat thinking, he heard a knock at his door. "Come in," he yelled.

Diamond strolled into his office. "Hey, baby," she sang in a happy voice as she shut the door behind her. "What's wrong?" She instantly recognized that something was wrong with her man, just from his demeanor, and the look on his face.

"I'm fine." Perry forced a smile on his face. "They need me downstairs or something?" he asked, wondering what she wanted.

Diamond pulled a pile of ten-dollar bills from out of her purse and laid them out on the table. "We need some singles downstairs."

"How many singles do you need?" Perry asked, opening up his change drawer.

"Five hundred."

Diamond slid down in between his legs while he counted out the singles.

"What you doing, baby?"

Perry tried to stop her from unzipping his pants, but she roughly slapped his hand away.

"Let me get that up outta you, baby," she whined, slipping his head inside her mouth. Diamond sucked on Perry's dick, bobbing her head a thousand miles per hour and moaning loudly.

Perry just sat back and watched as his baby took good care of him. This was the reason she was still alive. It was the little things that mattered to Perry. It seemed like every time her luck ran out, she did something to steal his heart away again.

"Baby, I want you to fuck my mouth."

Perry stood up and started to fuck Diamond's mouth like a jack rabbit, until he exploded in her. "Damn, baby!" he said, breathing heavily.

Diamond just smiled and took the singles from off the desk and went back downstairs.

Perry fixed his clothes before he sat back down. "Fuck!" He cursed as he buried his head in his hands. He was fighting a battle within himself, and was afraid of the outcome. He loved Diamond with all his heart, but wasn't sure if he could fully trust her yet. And on the other hand his hunger to kill needed to be fed, and fed soon, before he went crazy.

"Fuck this shit!" He grabbed his keys off his desk and headed downstairs.

Diamond saw Perry coming downstairs and met him at the end of the bar. "Hey, baby. You ready for round two already?"

"Nah, not yet, baby." He smiled. "I gotta go run home real quick." He kissed her lips. "I'm going to come back and pick you up before the club closes."

"Okay. Is everything all right?" Diamond asked skeptically.

"Yes, baby, everything is fine. Just gotta go grab some papers from up out of the safe, so I can finalize this new deal I'm working on," he lied.

"Okay, baby. Handle your business. I love you." Diamond kissed him again then watched him exit the club.

***

"Look at these clowns." Big Time laughed as him and Action Jackson cruised past one of Dirty Black's corners. Two workers stood on the corner selling drugs like it was legal, telling jokes, and loud-talking, showing their ignorance.

"These the type of niggas getting money now?" Action Jackson shook his head. "I must have been locked up too long."

"Word." Big Time double-parked directly across the street from the two hustlers.

Before Big Time even asked Action Jackson if he was ready, Action was already out the car and heading across the street with an M1 rifle in his hand.

When he reached the middle of the street, a woman screamed, "Oh my God! He's got a gun!"

Immediately everybody, including the two hustlers, took off running.

A smirk danced on Action Jackson's lips as he aimed his rifle at the whole crowd, pressed on the trigger, and waved his arms back and forth several times, hitting anything moving, including innocent civilians. Action Jackson didn't stop until the semi-automatic ran out of bullets.

Big Time sat behind the wheel with a smile on his face. He knew Action Jackson was a loose cannon, and he loved it. This was the perfect way to send a message to the streets.

Action Jackson jogged back to the car and hopped inside. Once he was back inside, Big Time put the pedal to the metal and burnt rubber.

"That's what the fuck I'm talking about," Big Time said, weaving in and out of the lanes on the highway.

"Let's get this money." Action Jackson sat his weapon on the backseat.

Since they were in jail together both men had been awaiting the day when they could get out and get back to business. Now that the time was now, neither man was going to let the opportunity slip through his hands.

Dirty Black sat behind his desk counting a huge stack of money. He then divided the money into two separate piles. "I got another job for y'all," he said, looking at Kendu and Amazon.

Kendu grabbed one of the piles of money and slid it in his pocket. He handed the other to Amazon. "What we gotta do?"

"You know that nigga Sky, right?" Dirty Black asked.

"You talking about that corny nigga from the Bronx, right?"

"Yeah, him," Dirty Black said. "I need y'all to get rid of that clown. He call himself getting a new supplier."

"Either he cop from us, or he don't cop at all," Amazon said, repeating the rules out loud.

"I need y'all to handle that for me tonight. Then we can go party with some sexy ladies."

"Let's go handle that now, 'cause I'm tired as fuck." Amazon stood up and stretched.

"Let's do it." Kendu and the two got up and headed out the door.

Outside Kendu hopped in the driver's seat, and Amazon slid in the passenger seat. Just as Kendu was backing out of the parking spot, he heard his cell phone ringing. He looked at his phone and saw Crystal's name flashing across his screen. "Yo', what's up?" he answered.

"Hey, what's up? You busy?"

"Nah, I'm good," Kendu replied. "I thought you had forgot about me for a minute."

"Never. What you doing tonight? I want to see you."

"I gotta take care of something right now, but you can swing by the crib later if you want."

"Text me the address, and I'll swing through around midnight."

"Sounds good to me," Kendu said. "I'ma text you right now," he said, ending the call.

After Kendu hung up, he realized no other woman had ever been to his house before. As he texted her his address, he thought about calling her back and telling her he wanted to meet up at another location. But it was something about her that he just liked, and she seemed like a real chick, so he decided to just go along with it.

Sky sat at his kitchen table inside his apartment along with two Jamaicans. Tired of paying Dirty Black's high-ass prices, he decided to deal with Maxwell.

Maxwell was a businessman who didn't take no shit. His dreads stopped at the middle of his back, and the scar on his face proved he had been in many battles. Sitting on his right-hand side was his partner Pete. Maxwell never went anywhere without Pete, and today was no exception.

"Hurry up, so we can go," Maxwell said in his thick Jamaican accent.

"You counted your money. Now let me count my pounds to make sure they all here," Sky said with an attitude. He couldn't stand Maxwell. The only reason he did business with him was because he had the best weed prices in town.

"Sit down and chill the fuck out!" Sky said, shaking his head. He took his sweet time looking through the duffel bag, just to fuck with Maxwell.

Right outside Sky's apartment. Kendu pulled out his .45 and placed his back up against the wall. He watched as Amazon pulled out two 9 mms and knocked on the door with the butt of the gun.

"Who the fuck is that?" Maxwell asked as he and Pete pulled out their guns and looked at Sky.

"I don't know," Sky replied in a whisper, tiptoeing towards the front door. He looked through the peephole and cursed silently when he saw Amazon standing on the other side of the door.

"Who the fuck is that?" Maxwell asked again.

Before Sky got a chance to answer, a loud blast erupted, followed by the front door being kicked open.

Amazon had shot the lock off the door then kicked it open. He quickly charged inside the apartment, popping shots.

Maxwell returned fire as he backpedaled into the kitchen. Sky froze up when he heard the loud, thunderous gunshots going off.

Kendu stood out in the hallway with his back still placed up against the wall. When he heard multiple shots ring out in the apartment, he immediately knew that whoever was inside was armed. As soon as the gunfire paused, he charged inside the apartment. The first person he saw was Pete, who was making a dash for the kitchen. He quickly sent two shots to his back, dropping him in his tracks.

Next, he turned his gun on Sky, who was still frozen like a deer caught up in some headlights. One shot to the head quickly put him to sleep forever.

Maxwell sprung from around the corner, sending reckless shots all over the place, forcing Kendu to take cover behind a nearby wall. Maxwell stood in front of the kitchen, letting off, until he ran out of bullets.

Once Amazon heard Maxwell run out of bullets, he immediately came from out of his hiding spot, and slowly walked towards the kitchen.

"I ain't got nothing to do with this shit," Maxwell said, trying to cop a plea. "I just came here to pick up my money from Sky."

Amazon gave the man a disgusted looked before blowing his brains all over the wall. "Come, we outta here," he said, and him and Kendu exited the apartment, leaving another unsolved murder for the cops to try and figure out.

Perry pulled into his garage and quickly shut the door behind him. He slid out the driver's seat and reached in the backseat, removed his mechanic suit, then put it on over his regular clothes.

He sighed loudly as he walked to the back of his car towards the trunk. The battle he was fighting within himself was taking a toll on his body. He had an urge to kill, and a taste for blood. He thought that, once he found a real woman, his thirst for blood would die, but he was wrong.

Inside his trunk lay a young lady he had kidnapped outside of his club. The young lady was doubled over between two cars throwing up when he crept up on her from behind.

He popped open the trunk, and immediately the woman tried to scream, but all that could be heard was a muffled noise, since her mouth was heavily taped.

"Nobody can hear you." Perry smiled as he grabbed the young lady and tossed her over his shoulder like she was a sack of potatoes.

He carried her throughout the house until he reached the basement door. "Home, sweet home." He chuckled as he opened up the door and headed down the steps.

Once down in the basement, he placed the young woman in a chair and quickly tied her up so she couldn't escape. The first thing he did was snatch the tape off of her mouth, along with any hair she had on her upper lip.

Instantly the woman threw up, obviously still feeling the effects from the alcohol she had consumed earlier.

"Where am I?" the woman asked, a long string of saliva hanging from her chin. "Where the fuck am I?"

"You're home," he said with a smile, removing a bag of tools from the closet.

"My friends are going to come looking for me," the woman said, trying to scare the man who had captured her.

"So let them come," Perry said seriously. He slipped his hands inside the latex gloves that the doctors use.

"What are you about to do?" the woman asked in a nervous tone. She threw up again.

"Dont worry. This won't hurt a bit." Perry turned around with two wire hangers that he had bent into the shape of a knife.

"Please don't," the woman said, endless tears on her face. "Why are you doing this?"

Perry ignored the woman as he roughly spread open her legs, taping the hangers both to the legs on the chair. That way she couldn't close her legs even if she wanted to.

He slowly rolled up her skirt then snatched the woman's thong off of her like the fabric was made out of tissue.

"I have money," the woman pleaded. "Just name your price and it's yours."

"Keep your money, sweetheart." Perry smiled as he roughly jabbed the wire coat hangers deep inside the woman's vagina, causing her to howl at the top of her lungs.

***

Back at the club Diamond sat inside Perry's office counting up the money they had made from the bar so far. She heard somebody knocking on the door and quickly placed the money inside the drawer. "Come in."

Cory stepped inside the office with a smile on his face. He was the one who ran the place whenever Perry wasn't there.

"What you smiling for?" Diamond started smiling herself.

"We cleaning up tonight," Cory said, talking about how much money the club had already made and the night wasn't even halfway over. "I need the key to the storage room 'cause we running out of liquor."

"I don't have the key," Diamond told him.

"Well then, who got it?"

"Perry has all the keys." Diamond pulled out her cell phone and dialed Perry's number. She listened as his phone rang out then went to voice mail. "He not answering." She redialed his number, only to get the same result. "He's not answering."

"So what we suppose to do?" Cory said, looking nervous.

"Fuck it. Gimme your car keys," Diamond said as she stood up from behind the desk.

He tossed her his keys. "What you about to do?"

"I got a copy of all the keys at the house in case of emergencies," she said as she headed out the office. "Which car is it again?" she yelled over her shoulder.

"The green Honda Civic," Cory yelled back as he made his way back downstairs.

Diamond hopped in Cory's car and searched through his CDs. "Yes." She found Alicia Keys' CD. She quickly popped it in and pulled out of the club's parking lot and headed home.

As Diamond drove, she wondered why Perry wasn't answering his phone. "He probably fell asleep," she said to herself.

She continued to sing along with Alicia Keys until she finally pulled up into the driveway. "I knew he was in here 'sleep," she said out loud, seeing the top of Perry's car in the garage.

Knowing she had to hurry up and get back to the club, Diamond quickly hopped out of the car and headed inside the crib. She made a beeline for the bedroom so she could surprise her man. Diamond stood in the doorway with a confused look on her face when she saw that the bedroom was empty. Where was Perry?

"Babbbbbyyyy!" she yelled as she headed back downstairs.

Perry circled the helpless woman in the chair like a shark that smelled blood. The woman begged him with her eyes to please stop, but he ignored her look as he backhanded her so hard, the chair almost tipped over.

A broad smile spread across his face as he removed a sharp butcher's knife. He got down on both knees and began to saw away at the woman's pinky toe. The sight of all the blood had turned him on.

Just as he was about to move on to the next toe, he heard his front door slam. "What the fuck!" he mumbled. He shot to his feet and listened closely to make sure he wasn't hearing things.

Seconds later he heard the stairs squeak as somebody was going upstairs. "Fuck!" He quickly snatched off his gloves and tossed them on the floor. Then he slid out of his mechanic suit. As soon as he got the suit off, he heard Diamond calling him.

Fuck is this bitch doing here? He hurried up the steps.

Perry made it upstairs and quickly shut and locked the basement door behind him. He turned around, and Diamond was staring dead at him.

"Oh! Hey, baby. What are you doing here?" Perry asked in a shaky voice.

"I had to come and get the spare key for the storage room in the club. I called you like five times, but you didn't answer the phone," Diamond said, looking at Perry suspiciously. "What was you doing down in the basement?" she said, her hands on her hips.

"The damn basement got flooded again," he lied.

"You must think I'm a damn fool," Diamond said, walking up to him. "You got another woman down there, don't you?"

"Huh?" Perry said, caught off guard. "Baby, you know I would never cheat on you."

"Oh yeah?" Diamond looked him up and down. "Then let me go down there and see for myself."

She reached for the knob on the basement's door, but Perry quickly grabbed her wrist with force. "I said the basement is flooded!" he said through clenched teeth.

"Take your fuckin' hands off me." Diamond snatched her arm away. She knew Perry was hiding a woman in the basement. She turned and slapped him across the face. "Have that bitch out of here before I get back!" she said, her finger pointed in his face.

All Perry could do was rub his face as he watched Diamond storm out the house and slam the door. He waited until he heard her pull out the driveway before he peeked through the window to make sure she had really left.

Once the coast was clear he headed back down to the basement. He had to clean up this mess before

Diamond got back home. He quickly grabbed the sharp knife and stabbed the woman repeatedly until he was sure she was dead. He then took the knife and carved the young woman's face up, like he did all his victims.

Diamond drove down the street like a madwoman. She couldn't believe Perry had the nerve to bring another woman into their home. She was starting to believe that all men were the same. At times like these, she missed her husband.

"You know what," she said to herself. "I think I'ma swing by the house, since I ain't too far from there."

She dropped off the keys then headed to her old house.

Ten minutes later Diamond pulled up to her old house and saw a strange car just pull into the driveway. Just then she saw a beautiful woman with the body of a stripper emerge from the car and walk up to the front door.

"This nigga told me he would never let another woman into our home," Diamond said to herself as she continued to look on. She watched as Kendu answered the door and let the woman inside. "Oh, hell naw!" she said out loud. She hopped out her car and headed towards the front door.

Kendu sat in the crib sipping on some coconut Cîroc, and Drake's album played in the background as he waited for Crystal to arrive. When he had finally made it home, it was 11:30 P.M., so he only had thirty minutes to change out of his bloody clothes and take a shower. Rocking some Sean John sweatpants, a wife-beater, and some house slippers, on one wrist he wore a nice expensive-looking watch, and on the other a diamond-studded bracelet. He was bobbing his head to the music when he heard a knock at the door. He flicked his wrist and looked at his watch, which read 12:13 A.M.

He opened the door and smiled when he saw Crystal standing on the other side looking sexy as usual. "Thanks for coming," he said, stepping to the side so Crystal could enter.

"Thanks for inviting me." Crystal looked around at Kendu's living room. "You was making it seem like you lived in a cardboard box or something."

"This *is* a cardboard box compared to your crib." Kendu smiled as he opened his arms for a hug. As he hugged Crystal, he made sure to look down at her ass that she couldn't hide even if she wanted to.

Crystal looked at Kendu's glass. "What you sipping on?"

"Cîroc. You want in?"

"You already know how we do," Crystal said, referring to how drunk they got at the lounge that night.

"Make yourself at home." Kendu headed to the kitchen to make Crystal a drink.

As he returned to the living room, he heard someone knocking on the door like the police. *Bang! Bang! Bang!*

"What the fuck!" Kendu said out loud as he handed Crystal her drink.

He grabbed his .45 from under the couch cushion and headed to the door.

Bang! Bang! Bang!

Kendu looked through the peephole and saw Diamond standing on the other side. He put the safety on his .45 as he slipped the gun in his pocket, and cracked the door. "Wassup?" he asked, peeking his head out the door.

"Don't *wassup* me!" Diamond pushed her way up in the house. Immediately she spotted Crystal sitting on the couch sipping on a drink. "Who the fuck is this bitch?"

"Listen," Kendu said, grabbing her arm, "don't come in here with that bullshit. This my peoples, and we just chilling."

Diamond looked at Kendu like he was insane. "Y'all just chilling?"

"We are not together anymore, so what's the problem?" Kendu said, still holding her back.

"Either you put the bitch out of our house, or I'ma do it!" Diamond yelled. "And I ain't playing."

Crystal hopped up off the couch and smoothly slid out of her heels. She sat her drink down on the coffee table and put her hair in a ponytail. "Why the fuck is you yelling all up in my man's face?" she said.

Once Crystal got close enough, Diamond swung around Kendu and hit her in her face. From there it was on. Kendu stepped out the way and watched as the two women got busy, grabbing one another's hair and going to work on each other, tearing up his house in the process.

Kendu let the two get it outta their systems before he stepped in and broke up the fight. He then roughly escorted Diamond outside. "What the fuck is wrong with you?" he barked. "Don't come over here fuckin' my shit up then go back to that other nigga crib and play house!"

"Fuck you!" She swung at Kendu, still caught up in her feelings.

Kendu quickly grabbed her arms and pinned her down on the hood of Crystal's Lexus. "We are not together anymore," he said, looking in her eyes. "You chose who you wanted to be with. You been living your life, now let me live mine."

"Get the fuck off me!" Diamond said, tears pouring down her face. She knew she was wrong for what she did, but she just couldn't stomach her husband fucking another woman. Something inside of her just wouldn't allow her to just look past that, whether they were together or not.

"I'm sorry." Diamond got up, wiped her face, and headed back to her car.

Kendu just looked on as he watched her walk to her car. He still loved her, but he wasn't just going to sit around and wait for her to decide if she loved him again.

After Diamond's car pulled off, Kendu went back inside. As soon he stepped foot back inside the house, the first thing he did was apologize to Crystal, who had a few scratches on her neck.

"No, I'm sorry. I should've kept my cool." Crystal sipped from her glass. "Sorry for messing up your house."

"It's okay. I wanted to re-decorate anyway," Kendu joked.

He went to the bathroom and returned with a warm wet rag. He sat beside Crystal, and gently applied the rag to her scratches.

"You know what would feel better than that rag?" she said in a seductive tone.

"What?" Kendu asked, tossing the rag on the coffee table.

Crystal whispered in his ear, "I think it would be better if you kissed my wounds."

That being said, Kendu leaned over and began to kiss and suck all over Crystal's neck. He then made his way to her lips, and their tongues intertwined in a slow dance.

Crystal stood up and slid out of her one-piece dress. She stood before Kendu wearing nothing but a black thong. Kendu stood up and removed his wife-beater, revealing his six-pack. As the two kissed again, he lifted her up, and she wrapped her legs around his waist as the two continued to kiss, while he carried her upstairs to the master bedroom.

Kendu laid Crystal down on the bed and quickly removed his pants and boxers, while he watched Crystal slide out of her thong. Crystal's thighs were so thick, and her ass was so big and juicy, he had no choice but to taste her peach.

She spread her legs as far as she could, and he placed his head between her split and licked and sucked all over her wet pussy, like it was the last time he would ever be with a woman again.

Crystal moaned as she wrapped her legs around Kendu's head and thrust her pussy farther in his mouth. She moaned loudly as she felt herself releasing in his mouth and on his face. She then pushed him on his back and straddled him.

Inside of Crystal felt like heaven. Kendu just lay back and watched as she bounced up and down on his dick, demanding that he come.

Kendu kissed Crystal passionately as he came inside her, and Crystal lay her head on his chest, and the two quickly drifted off to sleep.

Chapter 14

Kendu's sleep was abruptly interrupted when he heard his cell phone ringing in the middle of the night. He looked over at the digital clock on the nightstand. It said 4:25 A.M. He grabbed his cell phone. "Yo'," he answered.

"We got a problem," Amazon said into the phone. "Get down to the spot now!"

Kendu listened as the phone went dead on the other line. "Fuck!" He cursed as he slid out the bed and quickly got dressed. He kissed Crystal on the cheek, who was knocked out as he headed out the door.

Kendu hopped in his Audi and backed out of his driveway like a madman. He didn't know what was going on, but from the tone of Amazon's voice, he knew it wasn't nothing good.

Twenty minutes later Kendu pulled up to the front of the spot and saw about ten to fifteen goons standing out front, talking loud. Immediately he knew something bad had gone down.

He walked up and gave all the men he knew dap and made his way through the house. He saw Dirty Black and Amazon sitting in the back room talking. "What's going on around here?" Kendu asked as he gave both men dap.

"It's time to ride out." Amazon was dressed in all-black. He was tired of waiting around and ready to hurt somebody.

"This clown Big Time made a move on two of our soldiers," Dirty Black said in a calm voice. "Now him and his whole crew going to have to pay."

"So what's the plan?" Kendu asked, still a little shaken from being awaken from his sleep so suddenly.

Dirty Black sat straight up. "That clown you used to fuck with named Deuce, you still know where he lives?"

Once Kendu heard Dirty Black say Deuce's name, he knew he was going to have to kill his childhood friend. "Yeah, I know where he lives."

"Good," Dirty Black said. "He's the first one that has to go."

"Not a problem." Amazon tapped Kendu then headed for the door.

The ride to Deuce's house was a quiet one. Kendu didn't really have too much to say. He just never thought he would have to kill his childhood friend, a person who, when he was younger, had sleepovers at his home and all that.

Amazon noticed Kendu was in deep thought. "Fuck you over there thinking about?"

"Just ready to get this shit over," Kendu said, his eyes on the road.

Amazon laughed. "This shit is just now getting started."

"That's what I'm afraid of." Kendu pulled up across the street from Deuce's house.

Amazon hopped out the van and grabbed a shotgun from the back. He turned to Kendu. "You ready?"

Kendu threw his hood over his head and cocked back his .45. "I am now."

Deuce and Mousey sat up in his crib entertaining two of their lady friends. The foursome sat up talking, and getting their drink on.

"Yo', hold that thought," Mousey said as he got up and went to the bathroom.

"Yeah, that nigga always be having to take a shit," Deuce joked.

Just then Deuce's front door came crashing down.

The two women screamed at the top of their lungs when they saw the front door get kicked open and two hooded men barge in.

Immediately Deuce reached for his 9 mm that rested on the table, but a bullet in his shoulder from Kendu's .45 jerked his body back on the couch.

At first Amazon was going to let the women live, but he couldn't take all that screaming. He immediately aimed his shotgun at the first woman's face and pulled the trigger. *Boooooom!!!*

He then turned his shotgun to the next woman. *Booooooom!!*

Amazon cocked another round inside the chamber as he trained his shotgun on Deuce. "Where can I find Big Time at?"

"I—I d—don't know," Deuce stuttered.

Straightaway Deuce felt his knee get blown off from the force of the shotgun.

"I'ma ask you one more time." Amazon pumped another round into the chamber.

Out of nowhere Mousey came from out the back blasting his .357, firing recklessly over his shoulder as he dashed straight out the back door.

Kendu fired four shots in his direction, but missed all four as he watched Mousey escape out the back door. He then turned his .45 on Deuce. "Where the fuck is Big Time?"

"Why are you doing this?" Deuce asked, looking in Kendu's eyes. "We supposed to be family."

Kendu ignored Deuce's comments. "Last time. Where's Big Time?"

"Fuck you!" Deuce spat. "You never cared about me. You was always out for yourself. Do what you gotta do, 'cause I ain't telling you shit!"

Kendu shook his head at his friend's ignorance and disloyalty. He pulled the trigger, blowing his brains all over the back of the couch.

"Come on. We gotta go," Amazon said, and him and Kendu jogged back to the van.

Chapter 15

Crystal woke up in the morning and rolled over. She found out that she was alone in the bed. She quickly got up and got dressed. She had a wonderful time with Kendu last night, but she had a few things that she had to get done today, so she wrote him a note letting him know that she would call him later. She placed the note on his pillow as she left his house. Then she hopped inside her Lexus and headed home.

When Crystal pulled up in her driveway, the only thing on her mind was a nice hot shower. She stuck her key in the lock then entered her home. She tossed her keys on the counter like she always did, kicked off her shoes, and made her way to the living room. She stopped dead in her tracks when she saw Big Time sitting on her couch watching Rick Ross's new video on BET.

Big Time sat up on the couch, looking Crystal in her eyes. "Where the fuck you been all night?"

"None of your fuckin' business. What are you doing in my house? And how did you get in here?"

"This my house," Big Time reminded her. "Now I'ma ask you one more time—Where the fuck you been all night?"

"I been out. That's where I been! Now get out before I call the cops." Truth be told, Crystal would never call the cops. She hated them and everything they stood for. She was just hoping her threat would scare Big Time, but it didn't.

Big Time didn't want to have to put his hands on Crystal, but he couldn't have her just out all night with the next man. He had to do what he felt was necessary. He walked up to her and slapped her down to the floor. "Get ya ass up!" he growled. He dragged her through the house by her hair all the way upstairs to the master bedroom. "Bitch, you better have your ass at my house tonight, or else I'm going to kill you! And you better have my daughter with you." He punched her in the face so she could know he wasn't playing. "Let me not see y'all tonight." He left Crystal curled up on the floor crying.

Big Time exited Crystal's house, headed to his favorite soul food restaurant. He didn't want to hit her. All he wanted to do was show her that he had changed, and was ready to be a family man and treat her the way she deserved to be treated, but she refused to give him that chance. He loved Crystal and couldn't see himself without her, so he refused to let her leave and go be with the next man.

Kendu and Amazon cruised through every hood looking for Big Time and anybody affiliated with him.

"That was your first time killing somebody you knew?" Amazon asked, breaking the silence.

"Yeah," Kendu answered. "I just don't know why he would switch sides like that."

"Just because you loyal doesn't mean the people around you are too. I also had to learn that the hard way. This nigga Big Time still stuck in the eighties."

"Who the fuck is this Big Time nigga anyway?"

"Some clown who used to be the man back in the day, but what he has to realize is that the game has changed, and so have the players," Amazon said.

Kendu was about to say something else, until he saw flashing lights in his rearview mirror. "Fuck!" he cursed loudly. "Five-O behind us!" he announced in a panic tone.

"Damn!" Amazon said out loud.

"What we gon' do?" Kendu asked, placing his .45 on his lap. The van was filled with guns, duct tape, rope, and all kinds other shit they didn't have an explanation for. He didn't know what he was going to do, but he did know he wasn't going to jail.

"Fuck it! Speed up then stop," Amazon said. "We gon' have to take our chance on foot."

"Fuck it!" Kendu stepped on the gas, his eyes still on the cop car in his rearview mirror.

Amazon gave Kendu dap and looked over at him. "If one of us don't make it, I just want you to know you a real-ass nigga."

"You too." Kendu stomped on the brakes.

As soon the van came to a complete stop, both men quickly hopped out and ran in opposite directions. Kendu aimed his .45 at the cop car and sent three shots through the front window. Then he ran through someone's backyard, quickly hopped the fence, and disappeared through the woods.

Amazon ran in the opposite direction, through someone's backyard too. The only difference was, the officer decided to chase him.

"Fuck!" Amazon felt himself getting tired as he tried to escape through the woods. "Fuck this shit!" He turned around and fired two shots. When he looked up, he saw the officer fall to the ground. "Fuck!" He cursed. Then he thought, *Better him than me.* Amazon hit the main street, quickly hopped in a cab, and rode off to safety.

***

Kendu wiped down his .45 with the sleeve of his hoody. Then he tossed the gun in the woods along with the hooded sweater, before making his way to the main street and blending in with the crowd. He tried to catch his breath, but his walk was still swift.

Three minutes later he finally realized where he was. He wasn't too familiar with the area, but he knew it was a train station at the next corner. Kendu was just grateful that he got away from the police officer. He was hoping Amazon had as much luck as he did.

Just as Kendu spotted the train station, he saw Big Time exit some restaurant, carrying some food. "Damn!" He was hoping Big Time didn't see him.

Today must not have been his day, 'cause Big Time immediately spotted him and recognized him as the guy he saw hop in a cab at Crystal's house. He also remembered him at the cookout, standing next to Dirty Black.

From the evil smirk on Big Time's face, and the way he sat his food down on the hood of his car, Kendu knew something was about to go down. He instantly regretted tossing his gun in the woods.

Kendu was going to try to walk past him, but Big Time blocked his path with an ice grill on his face. Once the two got close enough, Kendu swung on Big Time. Big Time easily blocked the punch, using technique fifty-two that he had learned while in prison. He threw a quick jab that landed squarely on Kendu's nose, causing his eyes to water. He smiled as he blocked a few more of Kendu's punches.

Once Big Time got tired of playing with him, he dipped one of Kendu's punches and caught him with a clean uppercut, knocking him out cold. "Bitch-ass nigga!" He snarled, kicking Kendu in the face like it was a soccer ball.

Big Time looked up and saw that now a crowd had developed. A smile quickly appeared on his face. He pulled out his penis and urinated all over Kendu's face and clothes. Once that was over Big Time grabbed his food, slid back in his car, and bounced, leaving Kendu laid out on the ground.

Fifteen minutes later Kendu finally came back around. The only thing he remembered was bumping into Big Time, and that was it. He picked himself up off the ground and noticed that a nice-size crowd had formed.

"That nigga got knocked the fuck out!" he heard someone from the crowd say, which was followed by laughter.

Kendu touched his face, and his hand came away wet and sticky, smelling like urine. "What the fuck!" He thought out loud as his blood began to boil. Big Time had not only knocked him out, but he'd also humiliated him. As Kendu continued on towards the train station, he knew wherever he saw Big Time again, it was going to be on, on sight.

Big Time made it back to the hangout crib and couldn't wait to brag about how he had knocked out one of Dirty Black's boys, but when he got inside, he saw everybody standing around Mousey. "Fuck going on around here?"

"They just killed Deuce, and tried to take my head off!" Mousey said, a hint of fear in his voice.

"Who?" Big Time asked.

"Dirty Black's peoples," Mousey said. "About fifteen of them bum-rushed the crib, and they all had machine guns." He lied to make himself seem bigger than he really was.

"So how you get up outta there?" Big Time asked.

"I shot my way up out that bitch!" Mousey told him.

"Fuck it! These niggas wanna war, that's what they going to get," Big Time said, looking around. "Yo', Action, me and you going to go take care of Dirty Black tonight. The rest of y'all niggas, I want y'all out here on these corners getting this money."

Big Time and Action Jackson exited the crib. If Big Time knew that Dirty Black had his people try to take out his little nephew, he definitely would've killed Kendu right there in the middle of the street earlier.

"What's the plan?" Action Jackson slipped his hands inside his black gloves.

"We going to pay Dirty Black's ass a visit," Big Time said as they both hopped inside the ride. "But, first, I gotta go pick up my babies real quick and take them back to my crib," he added, headed towards Crystal's house.

Big Time pulled up in Crystal's driveway and hopped out the car. He had a serious look on his face as he banged on the door.

After three minutes of waiting, Big Time turned, lifted his leg, and kicked the door. It took two tries before the door finally gave in. Big Time and Action Jackson searched the crib like it had a hidden treasure.

After searching the house for over six minutes, he and Action Jackson came up empty.

"What you wanna do now?" Action Jackson asked.

"Let's go handle this business. I'll catch up with her later," Big Time said, and they exited the house.

***

Kendu hopped out the shower still upset that Big Time had pissed on him. He already had planned in his head what he was going to do to him the next time they bumped into each other. He dried off and threw on some sweatpants and a wife-beater. He thought about ordering some food, but his jaw was still a little sore from the beating he took earlier in the day.

"Fuck this shit!" Kendu cursed as he opened up a bottle Grey Goose and poured himself a shot. He downed the liquid fire in one gulp then poured himself another one. He downed the second shot and was about to pour a third, when he heard somebody knocking on his door.

"Who the fuck is knocking on my door at this time of night?" he said out loud. He grabbed the .380 he had resting on his countertop and headed towards the door.

Kendu opened the front door and saw Crystal and a little girl who he figured was her daughter standing on the other side with a bunch of luggage. The look on their face said that they didn't have any other place to go where that clown Big Time wouldn't find them. He stepped to the side, so Crystal and her daughter could enter his home.

As Crystal walked past him, she mouthed the words, "Thank you."

Kendu just replied with a head nod. "And what might your name be?" he asked the little girl.

"Jessica," she replied politely with a smile.

"Nice to meet you, Jessica," Kendu said, gently shaking her hand. "Make yourself at home. If you need anything, and I mean anything, you just let me know."

After Kendu got Crystal settled in, and Jessica ready for bed, him and Crystal sat on the couch cuddled up on one another.

"Thank you so much," she said. "I really appreciate this, and I promise I won't be here for long."

"Take as much time as you need, baby." Kendu noticed Crystal's busted lip and a small bruise under her eye. "What happened?" he said, nodding towards her busted lip.

"When I left here the other day," she began, "I went home, and that fool was already inside my house waiting for me. He started questioning me about where I was coming from, and when I didn't answer, he started hitting on me."

"You never have to worry about that clown putting his hands on you again," Kendu promised her. "I just bought this new movie earlier. You wanna check it out?"

"Sure." Crystal smiled. "What's the name of it?"

"It's called *No Way Out*."

"I would love to." Crystal curled up in Kendu's arms after he sat back down, and the two watched the movie.

Chapter 16

The past two weeks for Perry's and Diamond's relationship had been rocky. Diamond was still mad because she thought Perry had another woman in their home. And Perry was fighting his own demons. He fought with himself not to kill Diamond. He wanted to trust her, but something inside of him just wouldn't let him. It was something about her that he loved, and something about her that he didn't trust.

Perry walked in the bedroom, and saw Diamond laying across the bed butt naked watching TV. He was about to tell her something, but the sight of her nice plump ass just sitting right there messed up his train of thought.

"What?" Diamond asked, when she noticed he was looking at her.

Perry didn't reply. He just walked over to her and made her get on all fours on the bed. He spread Diamond's ass cheeks open and began eating her pussy from the back, knowing that was her favorite.

"Ooooh!" Diamond moaned, throwing her face in a pillow.

Perry licked and sucked all over Diamond's clit, forcing her to come hard. He smiled as he slapped her ass. "Now get up and get dressed," he told her. "We going out."

"Where we going?" Diamond was drained from the sexual episode.

"To go get something to eat," Perry answered as he started getting dressed.

An hour later Diamond stepped out the house wearing an all-red business suit, with her matching red pumps, her hair flowing in the wind as she walked to the car. Perry wore some slacks and a nice sweater.

"You driving," he said as he slid in the passenger seat of her all-black Audi A8.

For the whole ride to the restaurant, Diamond tried to make small talk, but she could see that his mind was somewhere else. "You all right, baby?"

"I'm fine, baby," Perry said, a fake smile on his face. "Just got a lot on my mind. Got a lot of paperwork I gotta fill out for the club."

Diamond pulled up in the restaurant's parking lot. "I'm here if you need me, baby."

Inside the restaurant, a waitress quickly escorted them through the restaurant over to their table. "Can I get y'all something to drink while y'all look through the menu?" she asked politely.

"Yes, can you bring us a bottle of red wine, please." Perry was about to say something to Diamond, but when he looked up, he saw Kendu and a fine woman being seated right across from them. "There go your boyfriend," he said.

"What are you talking about?" Diamond said, a confused look on her face. She turned around and saw Kendu and Crystal being seated right across from them.

Kendu sat down and gave her a head nod as him and Crystal picked up their menus. Crystal shot her an evil look before picking up her menu. Diamond rolled her eyes at Crystal before focusing back on her own menu.

"Do you still love him?" Perry asked, never taking his eyes off his menu.

Diamond didn't know where all this was coming from. "Huh? Love who?"

"Don't play stupid with me! Do you still love that muthafucka or not?"

"No, baby. I only love you," Diamond told him. "If I wanted to be with him, then I would be."

A smirk danced on Perry's lips. "I'm not even hungry anymore. Let's go."

Perry got up and left Diamond sitting at the table, and she quickly got up and followed behind her man.

"What is your problem?" Diamond asked Perry when she finally caught up with him in the parking lot.

"Just open the door," Perry said, not even bothering to look at her.

Diamond sucked her teeth as she unlocked the doors and hopped in the driver's seat. Before Perry could even get his seat belt on, she stormed out the parking lot like a bat outta hell. The entire ride was filled with silence as Diamond weaved in and out of lanes on the highway until the Audi finally made it to their driveway.

"Jealous muthafucka!" she mumbled as she stormed in the house.

When Perry stepped in the house, she let him have it.

"Listen, nigga. I don't know what kind of chicks you used to dealing with, but you need to get with the program. I've never disrespected you in any way. Now if you can't deal with having a bad bitch on your arms, then let me know now, so we can stop wasting each other's—"

A backhand slap to the face shut her up.

Perry smacked the shit out of Diamond then started to strangle her, both of his hands around her throat. "Bitch, you just don't know!" he snarled through clenched teeth. He slapped her a few more times until she hit the floor.

He then dragged Diamond through the house by her hair until he reached the basement door. He grabbed the doorknob and froze. "What the fuck are you doing?" he said, catching himself. He let go of Diamond's hair and headed upstairs, leaving her crying on the floor.

Perry went upstairs and slammed his bedroom shut. He was going crazy. Never would he let a woman speak to him the way Diamond just did. He flopped down on his bed and began to think. He loved Diamond, but he was starting to see she was just like all the other beautiful women he had killed. Right then and there, his mind was made up. He knew he was going to kill her.

Dirty Black sat behind his desk bobbing his head to the Papoose mixtape that flowed through the speakers as he counted money. He separated his big bills from the small ones. "You ready?" He'd counted out one thousand singles as him and Amazon got prepared to go to the strip club.

"I'm always ready to see some ass," Amazon replied.

Dirty Black grabbed his 9 mm and stuck it in his waistband as he stood up. He'd been so busy, he hadn't been out in a while. So tonight he decided to go out and enjoy himself, and some of his money.

Dirty Black stepped outside with his foam cup filled with Grey Goose and a pinch of orange juice in one hand. In his other, he held his cell phone up to his ear as he spoke to one of his many women. As him and Amazon strolled to Amazon's Range Rover, he looked over both shoulders before hopping in the passenger seat.

Amazon hopped in the front seat, popped a Young Jeezy CD in, then pulled out into traffic. "Did you ever holla at Kendu and see if he made it away from the police okay?"

"Yeah. I holla'd at him the other day. I gave him a few days off," Dirty Black told him. "He been putting in mad work. I don't want to drain him, you know."

"I can dig it." Amazon pulled up next to two fine women at the red light. Immediately his window rolled down. "Yo', ma, where y'all headed?" he yelled out the window.

"We about to go home," the passenger yelled back.

"Y'all want some company?"

The cars behind Amazon were beeping their horns, because he was holding up traffic now that the light had turned green.

"I don't think our boyfriends would like that," the passenger replied.

"I can respect that," Amazon said. "But I'ma give you my number anyway." He reached in his compartment and removed a piece of paper. He scribbled his number down and handed the paper to the passenger. "Holla at ya boy," he said with a wink.

He then turned to Dirty Black. "Look like she got a fat ass, right?"

"Couldn't really tell. She was sitting down. Her face was straight though."

"Yo', fam!" an angry voice barked, coming from Amazon's left. "You holding up the muthafuckin' traffic!"

Amazon looked at the man like he was crazy. "Nigga, don't you see me talking?"

"Fuck all that!" the man huffed. "Move this shit now, or it's going to be problems!"

Dirty Black smiled and looked at Amazon. "Handle your business."

Amazon hopped out the Range and fucked the man up like he was a woman. After he knocked the guy out, he stomped him out until his leg got tired, leaving the guy laid out in the street a bloody mess.

"Bitch-ass nigga got a lot of nerve," Amazon huffed as he slid back in the driver's seat and pulled off.

For the rest of the ride Amazon and Dirty Black laughed about how bad he had beat the man up in the middle of the street.

Ten minutes later they pulled up in the strip club's parking lot. Amazon quickly drove past two men talking to two women outside in the parking lot.

"Hold on. That looked like that nigga Big Time." Dirty Black turned around to get a better look.

Amazon slowed the truck down, so he could look too.

"I think that's him," Dirty Black said as he pulled his 9 mm from his waistband. "Circle this bitch. We gon' ride around and air this whole shit out."

Amazon sat his MAC-10 on his lap as he drove around the building.

Big Time and Action Jackson leaned up against his new white BMW talking to two off-duty strippers. "I'm saying, y'all trying to make some money tonight or what?" Big Time asked the ladies.

"How much money you talking about?" the dark-skinned stripper named Hershey asked.

"I'm saying we ain't no tricks or nothing, but we'll give y'all a couple dollars," Big Time countered.

The other stripper named Almond Joy asked Action Jackson, "You don't talk?"

"I talk," he said. "But y'all bitches ain't talking about nothing."

"Bitches?" Hershey echoed, rolling her eyes. "Don't disrespect us like that. We just out here trying get our money like everybody else."

"He ain't mean it like that, baby." Big Time noticed a Range Rover pull up into the club's parking lot. At first he didn't think nothing of it, but when he saw the truck slow down then circle around the building, he knew something was up.

He looked over at Action Jackson, who was on point, his hands on his twin .45s.

"Yo', come give me a hug," Big Time said, pulling Hershey close to him.

As soon as he saw the Range Rover bend the corner, he quickly threw Hershey in a choke hold from behind as he pulled his .40-cal from the small of his back and began firing at the truck.

Amazon and Dirty Black quickly ducked down as the bullets ripped through their windshield. Dirty Black quickly hopped out the truck and fired four shots in Big Time's direction before he took cover behind the Range Rover. Two of the four shots hit Hershey in the chest, killing her instantly.

Amazon aimed his MAC-10 at the two men from the driver's seat and let it spit, *Pat! Tat! Tat! Tat! Tat! Tat!*, firing shots from the inside of the truck.

Action Jackson ran through the parking lot popping shots from his twin .45s, not caring who he hit. When Big Time heard the machine gun ring out, he also took off running, ducking down behind cars.

Dirty Black sprung up from behind the Range Rover and sent five more shots in Big Time's direction.

"Yo', we out!" Dirty Black yelled as he hopped back in the passenger seat of the Range.

Once Dirty Black was back in the truck, Amazon threw the truck in reverse, and backed up out of the parking lot, going full speed.

When Action Jackson saw the Range Rover start to back up, he ran toward the truck popping shot after shot, trying to take off a head or two.

Once the Range Rover was out of sight, Action Jackson quickly turned to Almond Joy and popped her head off right in the parking lot, getting blood all over his face. She had seen his face, so she had to go.

Action Jackson then quickly jogged to the awaiting BMW just as people began coming out the strip club to see what had just happened. Big Time peeled off, leaving tire marks throughout the parking lot.

"I tried to take that nigga head off!" Amazon said as he pulled over on a side road. He hopped out the Range Rover. He removed all the papers from out of the glove compartment and wiped away all of their fingerprints before he abandoned the truck. It wasn't in his name, so he could care less.

Dirty Black reloaded his 9 mm before he left the Range, just in case they bumped into Big Time and his man again. "You got more bullets?"

"Nah, my shit empty," Amazon replied as him and Dirty Black walked over to the corner and flagged down a cab.

Kendu and Crystal sat at the kitchen table eating some steak and mashed potatoes that she had whipped up. "I'm so glad Jessica is over at my mom's house for the night." Crystal took a sip of wine.

"Can I ask you a serious question?" Kendu asked, looking down at his plate.

"Sure." Crystal gave him her full attention. "What's on your mind?"

"Your baby father, the next time I see him, I'm going to kill him. I just hope—"

"Let me stop you right there. I could care less about that jackass. Truth be told, if I could get away with killing him myself, I would."

"Music to my ears," Kendu said with a smile.

"But even though I care nothing about him, that doesn't mean I want to lose you in the process of getting rid of him."

"I ain't going nowhere, baby." Kendu grabbed her hands. "And I just want you to know that you never have to worry about that chump putting his hands on you again, you hear me?"

Crystal nodded her head yes. Then she leaned over the table and planted a few soft kisses on her man's face. She knew Kendu and Big Time would wind up clashing. She just prayed that, whatever went down, Kendu would end up the one on top.

"Come here," Crystal said as she finished her glass of wine.

Kendu walked around the table with a smile on his face. "What's up, baby?" he said, already knowing what she wanted.

Crystal returned his smile. Then she disappeared under the table, pulled Kendu's love tool from his shorts, and went to work. Kendu just threw his head back and stroked the back of Crystal's head as she pleased her man. Crystal sucked her man dry then sent him upstairs to bed.

The next morning Kendu woke up to his cell phone ringing off the hook. "Yo'," he answered in his sleepy voice.

"Yo', wake the fuck up and get down to the spot right now. It's on and popping!" Amazon hung up in Kendu's ear.

"Everything all right, daddy?" Crystal asked.

"Yeah, everything is fine," Kendu answered as he stretched. "Just gotta go handle a little business."

"Be careful."

"You already know."

Kendu got dressed in all-black then headed out the door. "I wonder what it is now?" he thought out loud as he hit the highway doing twenty miles over the speed limit.

Fifteen minutes later he pulled up to the spot, crowded with a bunch of goons ready to put in work. Kendu gave dap to the guys that he knew as he made his way to Dirty Black's office.

"Glad you could finally make it," Dirty Black said with a head nod.

Kendu helped himself to a seat. "What's goody?"

"Shit got crazy last night. Me and Amazon ran into that clown Big Time," Dirty Black said like it was nothing.

"Word? And what happened?"

"We had a muthafuckin' shootout," Amazon butted in. "What you think happened?"

Kendu was about to tell them that he too had run into Big Time, but he decided to keep it to himself. "A'ight, so what y'all need me to do?"

"We just got word on where one of these clowns' stash spot is at," Dirty Black told him. "I need you to go and hit that shit."

"How many people they got holding down the spot?" Kendu asked, massaging the bridge of his nose.

"Just one, I heard," Dirty Black replied.

"Who gave you this info?" Kendu asked.

"What the fuck difference does it make!" Amazon barked. "When it's time to go to war, you don't ask no questions, you just ride."

"I'm ready to ride," Kendu said. "I just like to know what I'm getting myself into before I jump out the window. Smell me?"

"I need you to go and bring me back that money," Dirty Black said in a cool tone. "I wouldn't send you on a suicide mission." He smirked.

Kendu left the spot with a nasty taste in his mouth. He didn't like going into things not knowing everything. He hopped in the car and just sat there for a second so he could get his thoughts together.

Crystal stood in the kitchen making herself some breakfast, when she saw Kendu walk through the front door. "Hey, baby. You hungry?"

"Nah. I need you to do me a favor," Kendu told her.

"Anything, baby. What's up?" Crystal asked, ready to hold her man down.

"Get dressed. I need you to take a ride with me real quick." Kendu watched Crystal disappear upstairs so she could throw some clothes on. Deep down he didn't want to bring her along with him on a job, but right now she was the only person he felt he could trust.

Five minutes later Crystal returned downstairs wearing all-black just like Kendu. "How I look?"

Kendu smiled. "You look wonderful, baby. Now come gimme a kiss."

The two kissed then headed out the door.

Crystal hopped in the driver's seat, while Kendu slid in the passenger seat and punched the address in the GPS. For the whole ride the two talked and laughed like two high-school sweethearts.

"Right here is good," Kendu said, pointing to the curb.

Crystal leaned over and kissed him on the lips. "Be careful, baby."

"I got you, baby," Kendu said, hopping out the car. He leaned his head through the window. "If you see anybody pull up who looks like they might be a drug dealer or anything like that, I need you to call me immediately, a'ight?"

"You got it."

Crystal watched Kendu walk towards the building and disappear inside, and immediately she began to worry.

Once inside the building, Kendu pulled his hood over his head. He took the stairs to the floor he was looking for. Soon as he came out the staircase, his .45 already in hand, he saw a young lady standing waiting for the elevator.

He smoothly crept up behind her, placing his gun to the back of her head. "Scream and I'll blow your brains all over this hallway!" he threatened as he escorted the woman down the hallway. "All I need you to do is knock on the door, and that's all." He pushed the woman in front of the door and stood over to the side.

The woman swallowed hard as she raised her fist and knocked on the door. *Knock! Knock! Knock!*

Kendu heard several locks on the door unlock. Once the door even cracked open, he quickly forced his way inside, bringing the woman with him.

"Get down on the floor right now!" he said with force as he watched the man wearing a do-rag do as he was told. "You too," he said, turning his gun on the woman.

Once the both of them were on the ground, Kendu pulled a roll of duct tape from out of his back pocket and quickly tied the two of them together back to back. He then quickly searched the whole apartment.

He found a duffel bag in the back room in the back of the closet, full of cash and two guns inside. "Jackpot!" he said out loud as he heard his cell phone ring. "Yo', what up?" he answered.

"You got company," Crystal said nervously into the phone.

"How many?"

"Three," she replied as she watched the three men enter the building.

Kendu quickly tossed the duffel bag over his shoulder and exited the apartment. He made sure he placed his hand in the pocket of his hoody, his hand on the trigger, as he made his way to the elevator. When the elevator arrived, he watched three men step off as he stepped on, and pressed for the lobby.

Once the elevator reached the lobby, Kendu quickly jogged out the building with a smile on his face. "Let's go," he said as soon as he hopped in the passenger seat.

"Damn! My heart feels like it's about to come out my chest," Crystal said as she hopped on the highway.

"I appreciate you holding me down back there." Kendu reached down in the duffel bag and handed her a stack of money.

Crystal refused to take it. "I didn't do this for no money."

Kendu quickly removed three more stacks from the bag and handed it to her. "This is our pay," he told her as she pulled up in front of their house. "Now go put that money in the house. I'll be back a little later, a'ight?"

Kendu headed back to the spot to drop the duffel bag off to Dirty Black.

Chapter 17

Diamond looked at her bruised face in the mirror and knew she had to leave Perry. The only problem was, she didn't have a place to go. She applied makeup on all her bruises on her face, covering them up the best she could. As she exited the bathroom in her bedroom, she saw Perry getting dressed, to head to the club.

"You all right?" Perry asked, his back turned.

"Yes, I'm fine," she replied as she turned up the volume on the TV to hear a report about another woman being tortured and brutally killed. "I hope they fuckin' catch this fuckin' psycho," she said in a disgusted tone as she rolled her eyes at the TV.

Perry just continued to get dressed as he whistled an old-school tune. "When we get to the club all I want is to have a few drinks," he told her.

Perry was in such a good mood, because tonight was the night he was going to kill Diamond. His mind was made up, and she had to go.

"Baby, can I have your keys? I think I left my purse in your car."

Perry tossed her the keys to his car. "Hurry up, 'cause we gotta get going." He continued to whistle.

Diamond stepped in the garage and quickly popped the locks to search Perry's car for her purse. "I know I left it in here somewhere," she said to herself as she popped the trunk. "Maybe he put in there." She searched the trunk.

Inside the trunk she found a duffel bag. Her curiosity getting the better of her caused her to open up the duffel bag. Diamond's mouth hung wide open when she saw what was inside the duffel bag—duct tape, all types of tools, and a few sharp knives. Also she found an album full of photos. As she flipped through the pages she saw that all the pictures inside were of women, some black, some white.

"Fuck this shit! I'm leaving this crazy muthafucka tonight," Diamond said to herself as she slammed the trunk closed. She didn't know why all those women's pictures were inside of a scrapbook, and she damn sure didn't plan on finding out.

Kendu walked up in the spot and handed Dirty Black the duffel bag.

"How did it go?" Dirty Black asked.

"A piece of cake. You need me to do anything else tonight?"

"Nah. Why? What you got planned for tonight?" Dirty Black asked.

"Nothing—about to go to crib and chill with my girl. Probably order some food, and watch a movie."

"I think I'ma do the same thing," Dirty Black said, liking how that sounded. "What you got planned for the night?" He looked over at Amazon.

"Fuck all that lovey-dovey shit." Amazon poured himself another drink. "I'ma probably hit up a club or something."

"A'ight. I'ma get up with y'all later." Kendu slapped hands with Amazon and Dirty Black as he made his exit.

Twenty minutes later Kendu stepped foot inside his house and saw Crystal laying across the couch wearing nothing but a red thong.

"Hey, baby. I was waiting for you to get here." Crystal hopped off the couch and slid in Kendu's arms. "I got everything all set up for us."

Crystal had planned a nice romantic evening for her and Kendu, since Jessica was already in her room 'sleep.

"What you got planned, baby?" Kendu said with a smile. From the look on Crystal's face he could tell that she had probably been planning this all day.

"Well, first you have to get out of them clothes."

Crystal went to the fridge and grabbed a bottle of wine, along with two wineglasses. When she turned around, Kendu stood in his boxers only.

"Okay, come on," she said excitedly. She opened up the patio leading to the backyard where the Jacuzzi was. Inside the water were red rose petals.

Crystal smiled. "You like it?"

"I love it, baby." Kendu watched Crystal hop her sexy ass up in the Jacuzzi first then followed her lead. The warm water and the massager jets inside the Jacuzzi was just what he needed.

"All I want you to do is relax and just enjoy tonight," Crystal said as she handed him a glass of wine.

Kendu sipped on his wine as he watched her tie her hair up in a ponytail then go down on him.

Perry stepped in the club, and immediately the heat and bass from the speakers slapped him and Diamond both in the face. As usual the club was popping, which meant it was packed.

Diamond snaked her way through the crowd, trying to keep up with Perry as he made his way upstairs to his office. When she finally made it upstairs, she knew she had to come up with a plan and do it quick.

"Come sit down and have a drink with me," Perry said as he twisted open the top on a bottle of coconut Cîroc, his favorite drink.

"I can't," Diamond replied.

"Why not?" Perry asked, a strange look on his face.

"Because I'm pregnant," she lied. "I been trying to wait for the right time to tell you," she said, laying it on thick.

"Are you serious?"

Diamond noticed he didn't look too happy about receiving the news. "Are you mad at me?"

"No, of course not," Perry said, forcing a smile on his face.

Really, Perry was disgusted because he wanted to kill her tonight, but now that she was carrying his child, he had to re-think things.

"I haven't been feeling too good all day, but I didn't want to say nothing. I'm sorry for just dropping this on you like this."

"It's okay," Perry said as he poured himself a drink.

Diamond pressed. "Is it okay if I go back home and lay down, 'cause I'm not really feeling too good? And this loud-ass music ain't making it no better."

"Yeah. Sure, baby, go get some rest. You want to take my car?"

"No, baby. I'ma just catch a cab." Diamond kissed Perry on the lips then made her exit.

Big Time and his crew stepped inside the club like they owned the joint. Each man in his crew was fresh, and definitely shining.

"Yo', let me get some bottles over here," Big Time said to the bouncer, as him and his crew piled into the VIP section.

Immediately Action Jackson and a few other goons invited a handful of women to party with them. The party went crazy when one of Drake's songs came blaring through the speakers. Big Time grabbed a tall, thick, dark-skinned woman by her waist as the two of their bodies flowed to the beat. While Big Time got his party on, a few of his goons started tossing money in the air, causing all the other partygoers to start going crazy trying to catch the bills.

Perry came downstairs to get a better look at was going on. "Fuck!" He hated drug dealers. To him they were so ignorant. He walked up to one of his bouncers and tapped him on the shoulder. "Keep a close eye on those animals. I don't want them to destroy my club." He headed back upstairs.

The bouncer just continued to look on as Big Time and his crew had a ball.

"Keep the change," Diamond said, handing the cab driver a fifty-dollar bill. She quickly hopped out the back of the cab.

Once inside the house Diamond quickly ran up the stairs to her closet. She grabbed a duffel bag and piled as many clothes as she could inside. Once it was full, she grabbed a book bag and went into Perry's closet and filled it up with his cash.

"This is for all the times you put your hands on me, muthafucka," she said out loud as she grabbed her two bags and made her exit.

Outside, Diamond tossed her bags in the trunk of her Audi, slid in the driver's seat, and backed out the driveway like a madwoman. She hopped on the highway and just drove. She had no place to go, but she knew she couldn't stay there any longer.

Chapter 18

Amazon pulled up in the club's parking lot with two soldiers, his music blasting. He slid out his truck looking like an animal, his rugged beard making him look older than he really was. On his feet he wore a pair of crisp construction Timbs, True Religion jeans, and a tight-fitting white thermal shirt, and his Yankee fitted sat at a forty-five-degree angle on his head. Him and the two soldiers he was with walked straight to the front of the line.

After talking to one of the bouncers, Amazon and the two men he came with were allowed inside the club. "This what the fuck I'm talking about," Amazon said, rubbing his hands together as he squeezed through the club over to the bar, bumping some girl in the process.

He ignored the woman's attitude as he ordered three bottles of Grey Goose. Amazon took a swig from the bottle before snaking through the crowd, headed for the dance floor.

The club went crazy when the Rick Ross song, "B.M.F." came on.

"I think I'm Big Meech, Larry Hoover" the whole club chanted.

When Big Time heard that song come on, he bobbed his head as a fine-ass Spanish chick moved her body like a snake in front of him. As he took a swig from his bottle of Rosé, he saw a cat that looked real familiar.

"Hold up!" Big Time pushed the Spanish chick out the way so he could get a better look. Once he was sure the man he was looking at was Amazon, a smile appeared on his face. He quickly notified Action Jackson on what was about to go down.

Amazon stood in the middle of the dance floor as two women sandwiched him with their asses as the trio grinded to the beat. In the midst of all the fun he was having, he looked up and saw Big Time and his crew headed in his direction. He quickly pushed both of the women off him.

"Hey, what the fuck is your problem?," one of the girls huffed.

Seconds later all hell broke loose. Big Time walked up on Amazon and swung on him.

Amazon blocked the punch and busted his Grey Goose bottle over one of Big Time goons' head. The two goons who came with Amazon immediately went head up with Big Time's soldiers.

In the middle of the dance floor Amazon and Big Time went at it like professional boxers from back in the day, both men landing vicious blows on one another, each man's pride and ego too big to submit, the whole time Rick Ross's voice booming through the speakers.

As the fight went on, Big Time caught Amazon with a right hook to the chin, causing the big man to stumble backwards. Amazon quickly regained his balance as he ran full speed towards Big Time and tackled him like a linebacker. The two men landed in the middle of the dance floor as the crowd shifted out of their way.

Perry came running down the stairs when he heard all the chaos. Just as he reached the dance floor, several bouncers were finally breaking up the brawl.

"Get these fuckin' animals the fuck up out of my club!" he yelled as he helped toss a few of the men out.

Once outside Amazon was still a little dizzy from the choke hold that the bouncer had him in as two of them escorted him out the club. He was about to head to his truck when he saw a man walking through the parking lot carrying an AK-47.

"What the fuck?" Amazon said out loud as he took off running.

Action Jackson walked through the parking lot holding his AK like it was a newborn baby. As soon as he spotted Amazon, he aimed the AK at him and let it rip.

Rat! Tat! Tat! Tat! Tat!

Action Jackson waved the AK in the direction that Amazon ran in, hitting anybody in the way. Women, men, bouncers, it didn't matter.

Amazon ran as fast as he could. Once he heard the AK ring out, he started running in zigzag fashion. He felt a bullet rip through his shoulder then the back of his thigh, and his big body hit the ground and slid across the concrete.

Action Jackson popped a fresh clip in the base of the assault rifle as he moved in for the kill, but two uniformed cops interrupted his plans. He looked at the cop car pull up and come to a complete stop. Immediately he aimed the AK at the cop car and squeezed the trigger.

"Come on, we gotta go!" Big Time grabbed Action Jackson and pulled him towards the getaway car that awaited them.

***

Kendu and Crystal sat on the couch sipping on wine and just chit-chatting to the sounds of Alicia Keys flowing through the surround-sound system. Kendu sat at the end of the couch massaging Crystal's feet, while she went on telling him about her and Big Time's past. Kendu couldn't believe how bad Big Time had treated her, but at the same time he was thankful, because if he hadn't treated her that way, the two of them wouldn't have been together right now.

"Well, I just want you to know that you never have to worry about being treated like that ever again," he told her.

"I know, baby." Crystal refilled her glass with some fine wine. She felt as though her prayers had been answered when she'd met Kendu. For the first time in her life, her relationship just felt right. "I love you."

"I love you too, baby." Kendu heard somebody knocking on his door with authority. He quickly looked up at the clock on the wall. It read 3:15 A.M.

"Who the fuck is knocking on my muthafuckin' door at this time of night?" Kendu said out loud as he grabbed his .45 from off the coffee table then headed towards the door. He looked through the peephole and immediately lowered his gun.

Kendu opened the door and saw Diamond standing on the other side with two bags with her. Just by looking at the bruises on her face, he already knew what time it was. "Come in," he said, stepping over to the side so she could come inside.

"Sorry for coming by so late."

"What are you doing here?"

"I need somewhere to stay, and I don't have nowhere else to go," Diamond told him.

"I have no problem with you staying here," Kendu told her. "But I don't live by myself anymore," he said, looking over at Crystal.

"Please, I have nowhere else to go," Diamond looked over at Crystal.

"Girl, come on in," Crystal said, waving her in from the couch. Even though Crystal didn't care too much for Diamond, the look on Diamond's face was the same look she had on hers when she had asked Kendu, and her daughter if she could stay with him, so she totally understood the situation.

"Thank you so much." Diamond ran over and hugged Crystal tightly. "I'll even sleep on the couch if I have to."

"That won't be necessary," Crystal said. "You can take the extra room."

"Hold on, hold on," Kendu said. "I need to know everything that's going on."

Diamond sat down and explained everything from how Perry beat on her, to how he always kept his basement locked. She even told them about the money she had stolen from him.

"Damn! That's crazy," Crystal said, shaking her head.

"That's not even the half of it. I also think he's the serial killer that the cops been lookin' for on the news."

"Do you have proof?" Kendu asked.

"No. But I found a bag in his trunk full of pictures of different women. I think those were his past victims."

"A'ight. Get you some rest tonight, and tomorrow we will come up with a plan."

Kendu watched Crystal show Diamond through her own house towards the empty bedroom. Of course, Diamond didn't like it, but what other choice did she have? Besides, she was grateful to have a place to rest her head, and somebody close by that she knew would protect her.

***

When Perry stepped foot in his home, immediately something didn't feel right. The house was way too quiet. He ran up the steps, skipping two at a time.

When he made it inside his bedroom and saw his closet door left wide open, he knew Diamond had left him. A devilish smile quickly appeared across his face as all kinds of sick and twisted thoughts raced through his mind. He slowly walked down to the kitchen and poured himself a shot of vodka. He sat in the dark thinking about how stupid he was for believing that Diamond would be any different from any of the other women he had murdered.

"Silly me," he said to himself. He tried his hardest to remain calm, but this was the first time Perry had ever let a woman get this close to him. Now Diamond was going to have to pay for that. With her life.

The next morning Kendu woke up to his phone ringing off the hook. He reached over on his nightstand, his eyes still closed, until he felt his cell phone. "Hello?"

"I need you over here ASAP. It's an emergency."

He recognized Dirty Black's voice. "You need me there right now?"

"Right now!" Dirty Black ended the call.

"Fuck!" Kendu cursed as he stretched. He slipped out the bed and quickly threw on the same clothes he wore the night before. He kissed Crystal on her cheek then headed downstairs.

When Kendu made it downstairs, he saw Diamond on the couch watching TV. "What you doing up so early?" he asked as he went to the fridge to grab himself some orange juice.

"I couldn't sleep. Got too much on my mind."

"You gon' be all right," Kendu told her.

"Don't worry. I won't be here for too long. I know you two need y'all space," Diamond said. "I don't want to come in between that."

"You fine. Take as much time as you need."

"Thanks. I really appreciate it." Diamond watched Kendu walk out the front door. She realized that she should have never left him from the beginning. That mistake she would have to live with for the rest of her life.

Kendu walked in Dirty Black's office, and by the look on his face, he knew something bad had happened. "What's good?" Kendu gave Dirty Black dap then took a seat.

"These niggas must die!" Dirty Black slammed his fist down on his desk.

"What happened?" Kendu asked.

"They caught Amazon slipping. Got him laid up in the hospital. Word on the streets is, some clown named Action Jackson clapped him up."

"Action Jackson?" Kendu echoed.

"Yeah, he supposed to be some big action freak or something like that." Dirty Black smirked. "I'm gunning for him personally."

Kendu sat there while Dirty Black gave him the rundown on everything going on. He was really taking Amazon being in the hospital hard.

"Whatever you need me to do, just let me know," Kendu said.

"You seen those three soldiers sitting outside?"

"Yeah," Kendu said, remembering seeing them on his way in.

"I got word on where this clown and his crew hang out at," Dirty Black said. "I need you to ride over there and let them know what time it is."

"Not a problem." Kendu got up and walked out into the hallway to inform the three soldiers on what was up. Now that Amazon was in the hospital, Kendu was Dirty Black's right hand.

Kendu stepped outside and took charge. "All I need y'all to do is follow my lead," he began. "It's broad daylight, so we just going to do a simple drive-by." And he and the three soldiers all climbed inside the old Chevy and headed out.

The ride was a quiet one. Kendu stared blankly out the window as the Uzi rested on his lap. A million thoughts ran through his mind as he sat in the backseat, but now was not the time to be worrying and thinking about other shit.

Once the Chevy got close to their destination, Kendu tied a red flag around his face to hide his identity. "Slow this muthafucka down," he said from the backseat as he rolled down his window. He spotted the house he was looking for and saw at least ten to twelve people on the porch.

Without hesitation, he stuck his Uzi out the window and squeezed the trigger, along with another soldier who rode along in the car.

· Action Jackson stood on the porch shirtless talking to a well-known freak from the neighborhood, while a few other goons sat on the porch playing spades.

The young lady admired the two chains that hung around his neck as he spoke. "That is unnecessary," Lisa said, touching Action Jackson's chains.

"I worked hard to be able to wear this," he told her.

"You ain't scared that somebody might try to rob you?" she asked.

"I'm willing to die for this." Action Jackson looked down at his chains that hung around his neck. "Besides, I keep something that will make a nigga think twice about taking anything from me." He nodded towards his SKS rifle that rested by his chair.

As Action Jackson stood on the porch talking to Lisa, he noticed an old-school car coasting down the street. Immediately he knew it was on. He quickly grabbed his SKS from the side of the chair as a loud series of gunshots rang out in broad daylight.

Kendu watched his bullets rip through several soldiers that stood on the porch. He waved his arms back and forth, trying to hit anything moving.

Warm blood splashed on Action Jackson's face as he saw Lisa laid out face down in the grass. Action Jackson jumped off the porch as he pressed the trigger on his assault rifle. The gun rattled in his hands as shells popped out the chamber back to back.

Kendu quickly took cover in the car as the bullets from Action Jackson's gun riddled and rocked the car. "Punch this shit!" he yelled out to the driver.

Action Jackson watched as the Chevy bent the corner. Immediately he ran to his car and tossed the SKS in the backseat as he hopped in the driver's seat and left the murder scene.

Dirty Black sat in his office getting his drink on, in deep thought. Ever since him and Big Time started beefing, he had to shut down a few of his spots due to the heat coming from the police. The cops didn't mind drugs being sold in the black community, but when bodies started dropping, and people started getting killed, that's when it became a problem.

While Dirty Black poured himself another drink, he heard his cell phone ringing. He looked at the caller ID and saw that the caller had blocked their number. Usually he didn't answer private numbers, but this time he did. "Who this?" he answered.

"Wassup," the voice on the other end spoke.

"Who is this?" Dirty Black asked again.

"Big Time. We need to talk."

"About?"

"This war has got to stop," Big Time said. "I'm losing too much money over this shit."

"Well, you should've thought of that before you decided to play tough," Dirty Black said coldly.

"Listen," Big Time told him, "I know your pockets are taking a hit as well, so I'm inviting you to my restaurant for a sit-down. All of this killing has got to stop."

"A sit-down?" Dirty Black didn't fully trust Big Time enough to have a sit-down with him yet, but he also knew that in order to keep the money raining in, this may have been the only option. "Text me the address, and I'll swing through."

"Okay, we can meet up tomorrow night around nine P.M.," Big Time said, ending the call.

When Kendu walked in the house, he was shocked to see Diamond and Crystal sitting on the couch having a drink while they watched *The Real NBA Housewives*.

"Hey, baby." Crystal got up and hugged and kissed her man. "How was your day?"

"Long." Kendu asked Diamond, "How you feeling today?"

Diamond replied with a smile. "Much better,"

"That's what I like to hear."

Kendu poured himself a drink. Before he could even take a sip, he heard somebody knocking on the door. *Who the fuck could this be?* he thought as he walked over to the door and opened it. His good mood went straight out the window when he saw Perry standing on the other side of his door.

"What the fuck you want?"

"I'm here for your wife," Perry said, looking Kendu in his eyes. "Now where is she?"

"Let me tell you something." Kendu took a step closer. "Next time you ever knock on my door, you are going to get shot. Understand? I'm going to let you slide this time because I'm in a good mood."

Kendu went to close the door, but Perry's boot stopped it from closing.

"I need to speak to Diamond now!"

Kendu quickly pulled his .45 from the small of his back and placed it underneath Perry's chin. "Nigga, what I just say? Get the fuck up outta here before I turn your head into velvet!" He shoved Perry out of his doorway.

"Diamond, I'm coming for you!" Perry yelled loud enough so Diamond could hear him. He smiled at Kendu, before turning and heading towards his car.

Kendu stood in the doorway until Perry's car was no longer in sight. "This clown gon' make me kill him," Kendu said as he closed and locked the door behind him.

Diamond stood up. "I'm about to leave. I don't want to bring no trouble to y'all."

"Fuck that! You don't have to go nowhere," Kendu told her. "If that clown come back, I'ma shoot him out his fuckin' shoes."

"I told y'all he was crazy," Diamond said, a nervous look on her face. She knew how crazy Perry was and what he was capable of. She didn't have proof, but she had a strong feeling that he was the serial killer from the news. And the last thing she wanted was to be his next victim. "I don't trust him," she said out loud.

"Tell you what," Kendu said, pulling a small .380 from his pocket. "Here. I'll keep this in the house, just in case that clown tries to come back when I ain't home." He sat it down on the counter.

"If he knows what's best, he better stay the fuck from around here." Crystal finished off her drink. "'Cause I ain't got time to be playing with no psychos."

"He acting like a psycho, until somebody knock him the fuck out!" Kendu said, and he disappeared upstairs so he could take a shower, hoping that would calm him down.

Perry drove away with a smile on his face. Not only was he going to kill Diamond, but now Kendu and Crystal were added to the list.

He pulled up in his driveway and quickly turned the car off. Once he stepped foot inside his house, he made a beeline for the basement. He had to whip up something special for Diamond. Something that she nor the media would ever forget.

Chapter 19

Dirty Black parked his Navigator in the parking lot of Big Time's restaurant. A sit-down was the last thing he wanted, but money came first in his life, so he had to do what he had to do. "You ready?" he asked, looking over at Kendu, who sat in the passenger seat.

"Let's do it." Kendu hopped out the truck.

Altogether, it was four of them heading inside Big Time's restaurant. As the foursome entered the restaurant, they were met by a huge six-foot-seven bodyguard.

"Nobody is allowed past this point without being searched," the bodyguard's voice boomed.

"Fuck outta here!" Dirty Black looked the big man up and down. "You better tell that nigga Big Time to come out here before I air this whole shit out!"

The big bodyguard gave Dirty Black a mean look before he left and went to go get Big Time.

Big Time came bopping toward the front of the restauarnt. "Gentlemen," he greeted them. "Glad y'all could make it. Right this way," he said, escorting the foursome upstairs to a booth reserved for his VIP customers.

When they made it upstairs, already seated at the table was Action Jackson and Mousey, while another seven-foot bodyguard stood looking over everything.

Once everyone was seated, Big Time began. "Glad y'all could make it. I called y'all down here because all the killing has got to stop, if we want to continue to make any money."

Kendu stared a hole through Big Time's face as he spoke. He so badly wanted to jump over the table and blow his brains all over the wall, but he had to keep his cool. He still hadn't forgot what Big Time did to him and couldn't wait until he got a chance for some payback.

"Listen," Big Time continued, "we going to have to share real estate. Your peoples stay off our corners, and my people will stay off your corners. That's the only way this thing is going to work."

"I don't know about this," Dirty Black said, pouring himself a drink.

"What's not to know about it?" Big Time asked. "We both in this thing to make money, right? And the only way we going to continue to make money is if both sides chill."

"My main man is laying up in the fuckin' hospital right now." Dirty Black looked over at Action Jackson, who had a smirk on his face. "And I'm telling you right now you better wipe that fuckin' smirk off your face before I do it for you!" Dirty Black shot to his feet.

Action Jackson didn't even flinch as he stayed seated. "If you think that was something, you're going to love what I'm going to do to you," he said.

"Do it now, you pussy!" Dirty Black's hand slipped down towards his waist.

That last comment caused Action Jackson to slowly rise to his feet. He reached for his waistband, but Big Time quickly stopped him. "Not in here."

"Fuck this shit! We out." Kendu draped his arm around Dirty Black's neck, and the foursome made their exit.

"Fuck!" Big Time cursed loudly.

"Fuck that punk-ass nigga!" Action Jackson said, waving him off. "Fuck them niggas! I ain't with all this sit-down shit anyway."

Big Time shook his head. Now that his attempt had failed, it was only one thing left to do. "You want him?" He looked over at Action Jackson. "You got him."

"About fuckin' time," Action Jackson said with an attitude.

"Make it quick. The faster Dirty Black is out of the picture, the faster we can go back to getting this money." Big Time sat back down at his table and poured himself a drink.

He'd tried to settle things the grown-up way, but that didn't work. And he knew Dirty Black wouldn't stop until one of them was dead. If everything went according to his plan, though, then it would be Dirty Black getting killed instead of him.

Dirty Black drove in total silence until he finally arrived back at the spot. "Y'all niggas, go get some rest tonight, 'cause tomorrow it's on," he announced.

Kendu knew the look he saw in Dirty Black's eyes. All the games were over now. Someone had to die, point-blank. "I'm out. Call me tomorrow." He slapped five with Dirty Black then hopped in his car and headed home.

Perry sat in a low-key car right across the street from Kendu's house. He had been staked out there all day just watching the house. He still couldn't believe that Diamond had got away from him before he got a chance to have his way with her. That right there was what ate at him the most. He felt as if she had used and outsmarted him.

As he continued to watched the house, he saw a Benz pull into the driveway, and out stepped Kendu. Just the sight of him made Perry's blood boil. He wanted to run down on him and murder him on sight, but he knew that in order to pull off his plan, he would have to wait for the perfect time. He had something real special for everyone who resided inside that house and couldn't wait until the perfect time to strike.

Kendu walked in the house and saw Diamond laying across the couch half-naked, looking sexy. "What up?" he said coolly as he walked over to the fridge.

"How was your day?" Diamond got up and walked in the kitchen with him.

"It was a'ight. Where's Crystal?"

"She's upstairs sleeping. I don't think Jessica was feeling too good. I think her stomach was hurting."

Kendu poured himself a glass of wine as he listened to what Diamond had to say.

"I want to thank you again for letting me stay here," Diamond said. "Especially after how I acted the last time I was here." She was embarrassed by her actions.

"It's all good." Kendu sipped on his wine. "I wouldn't just let you be out on the streets like that. You are still technically my wife," he reminded her.

Diamond smiled. "Are you hungry?"

"Nah, I just ate," he lied, afraid that Crystal would come downstairs at any moment and make their conversation out to be more than it really was.

Diamond laughed as she shook her head. "You never was a good liar," she said, digging in the cabinet and removing a frying pan.

Kendu sat on the stool as he sipped on his wine. He watched as Diamond worked her way around the kitchen that she knew so well, frying him some chicken.

The two ate fried chicken and sipped on wine until Kendu went upstairs and retired in the bed.

Chapter 20

Dirty Black stood in his office staring at the notepad in front of him with an address scribbled down on it. One of his stripper girlfriends had just contacted him and informed him that Mousey was in the club, drunk out of his mind, tossing money around like it grew on trees.

Dirty Black would've loved to see the look on Mousey's face before he got killed, but tonight he had to pick Amazon up from the hospital. So Kendu had the honor of taking Mousey out.

Kendu walked through the front door of Dirty Black's office dressed in all-black. "What it's looking like?" he asked with his signature smile as he gave the man who sat behind the desk dap.

"Got another job for you," Dirty Black told him. "This clown Mousey is downtown at The Golden Lady. I need you to cancel his contract for me tonight."

"He's there right now?" Kendu asked excitedly. Since day one, he'd never liked Mousey and couldn't wait to put his hands on the man.

"Right now." Dirty Black watched Kendu head out of his office in a flash.

Kendu got outside and quickly hopped behind the wheel of his car and sped off. He was in such a hurry to finally get rid of Mousey, he hadn't even noticed Action Jackson over in the cut a few blocks down on his bike.

Action Jackson kept a close eye on Dirty Black's spot as he continued to patiently wait for his target to show his face. He was tired of playing around with Dirty Black and planned on ending his life tonight.

Dirty Black rubbed the top of his head with his hand as he stood to his feet. He grabbed his P89 off his desk and stuck it in his waistband. He turned off the light and grabbed his foam cup that was filled with vodka as he made his way out the front door. He stepped outside and looked around as he took a sip of vodka before heading to his ride. His black Lamborghini sat untouched in the parking spot he left it in.

Dirty Black hit a button on his keychain and watched as the butterfly doors on his Lambo opened up for him. He sat his foam cup in the cup holder as he made the car come to life and pulled off like he was in a hurry.

When Action Jackson saw the Lamborghini pull off, he immediately revved his engine as he began to follow his target. His black helmet and dark visor hid his identity as he flew down the street like a madman. Up ahead the Lambo slowed down for a yellow light. Instantly Action Jackson pulled out his 9 mm with the infrared beam on top.

Dirty Black sat at the red light checking out one of the new features on his iPhone when he noticed a red beam on his windshield. "What the fuck!" He quickly ducked down when he heard shots blasting through his back windshield.

Dirty Black stomped on the gas pedal, and the Lambo roared and flew through the intersection. "Muthafucka wanna play," he said out loud. He made a sharp right onto the highway. He peeked through his rearview mirror and saw the gunman on the bike speeding up. Dirty

Black smirked as he sat his P89 on his lap and quickly switched lanes, flooring the Lambo. "Let's see if you can keep up, mufucka!"

Action Jackson swerved in and out of lanes, doing about ninety-five miles per hour, trying to keep up with Dirty Black. He watched as the Lambo weaved effortlessly from lane to lane. The Lamborghini had to be going at least 115 mph.

Dirty Black flew down the highway like a NASCAR driver. At the perfect time, he quickly made a sharp right and exited off the highway.

"Fuck!" Action Jackson had to lean so low to the ground, his right knee scraped the ground as he exited off the highway right behind the Lambo.

Luckily for Dirty Black, when he came off the exit, the light was green.

Action Jackson sped and aimed his 9 mm at Dirty Black's back tire and pulled the trigger. It took him four shots to finally hit the back tire.

"Ooooh shit!" Dirty Black yelled as he felt the Lambo spin out of control and hit a light pole. His head bounced off the steering wheel, but he remained conscious. He quickly hopped out the car with his P89, letting off shot after shot at the gunman on the bike.

Once the gunman was out of his sight, Dirty Black tried to run back to his Lambo, but he collapsed from the pain in his leg. He touched his thigh, and his hand came away bloody. "Fuck!" He tried to army-crawl back to his car, which was only a few feet away, but before he could make it, two cop cars came to a screeching stop behind him.

"Drop the weapon now!" one of the officers yelled.

Dirty Black dropped his P89 and surrendered. The officer roughly handcuffed him then painfully pulled him up to his feet, and tossed him in the back of the squad car. He slammed the door and went to join the other officers in searching the Lamborghini.

"Shit!" Dirty Black cursed as he sat bleeding in the backseat of the unmarked car. He watched as the officers searched his car looking for anything they could find. At that very moment he knew he had just fucked up, and the chances of him being released were slim to none.

Kendu sat in the strip club's parking lot waiting for his victim to exit the club. After sitting in the parking lot for an hour and a half, he couldn't take it no longer. "Fuck this shit!" he huffed. He stashed his .45 under his seat and hopped out of his vehicle and made his way towards the club's entrance. He tapped his boot to make sure his knife was where he always kept it.

The bouncer at the door gave Kendu a quick pat-down, just making sure he wasn't carrying a gun then allowed him to enter. Kendu stepped inside the strip club and quickly grabbed himself a drink as he scoped out the joint looking for Mousey. After two minutes of searching, he spotted the man he was looking for over on the other side of the club.

As Kendu sat chilling, he felt someone tap him on his shoulder. He turned around and saw Kiki standing in front of him.

"Hey, what's up?" Kiki said, giving him a hug. "Remember me? I met you at Dirty Black's cookout."

"How could I forget?" Kendu took a look at Kiki's ass, which looked even bigger, now that all she wore was a thong.

"I'm the one who called Dirty Black." Kiki straddled Kendu and grinded up on top of him, telling him everything he needed to know without it looking suspicious.

"I heard about what's been going on out here between y'all."

"I'm just here to handle my business," Kendu said, palming Kiki's ass, the whole time his eyes never leaving Mousey.

"Just make sure you're careful," she whispered in his ear.

"I got you." Kendu saw Mousey get up and head to the restroom. "Pardon me for one second, ma." He politely stuffed a twenty-dollar bill in her bra and smoothly headed to the back, where the bathrooms were.

Kendu slid his hand in his boot and removed his knife as he entered the bathroom. He flicked the blade out.

Mousey quickly turned around when he heard the sound of a knife being flicked open. "What the fuck!" he said when he saw Kendu blocking the doorway with a knife in his hand. "Somebody help!" he yelled, sounding like a bitch.

Immediately Kendu charged Mousey and plunged the knife in and out of his chest and stomach until he collapsed right there on the bathroom floor. Kendu cleaned his knife off at the sink before he slid it back in his pocket and exited the bathroom. He smoothly walked through the club like nothing had happened. He had to make his exit quickly due to all the blood on his shirt..

"I'ma catch you later," he whispered in Kiki's ear, smacking her on the ass as he left the strip club. Once out in the parking lot, he jogged to his car and quickly fled the scene.

When Kendu made it home he saw Diamond, Crystal, and Jessica all up sitting on the couch. "What's wrong?" he asked.

"Baby, go to your room." Crystal watched Jessica head upstairs to her room.

Once Jessica was out of earshot, Diamond spoke up. "It's Perry. He's been calling the house every thirty minutes."

Kendu took a seat next to Crystal on the couch. "What he said when he called?"

"He's not saying nothing," Diamond said. "We can just hear him breathing on the other end."

"You sure know how to pick 'em," Kendu joked.

The news reporter came on TV, talking about another woman's body was found behind a Taco Bell not too far from their house. The woman had been drowned, and her face badly cut up.

"I know it's him. I know it," Diamond said, looking at the TV. "I'm about to leave," She looked spooked. "I don't want to bring trouble to this house, especially while y'all have the little one here."

"I wish that nigga would come here and try that crazy shit," Kendu said, already thinking about what he would do to the man if that day ever came.

His thoughts were shattered when he heard the house phone ringing. Kendu saw both Crystal and Diamond staring dead at him. He quickly got up and walked over to the phone. "Who the fuck is this?" he answered.

No answer came back on the other end, just dead air.

"Listen, you pussy, the least you can do is be a man and talk!" Kendu yelled into the receiver before hanging up. "Tomorrow I'm going over to his house and pay him a little visit."

"It's not even worth it," Diamond told him, not wanting him getting into any trouble over her and her problems.

"Fuck that! I'm tired of playing with this clown!" Kendu huffed as he trotted upstairs.

"Please try to calm him down. I don't want him getting into any trouble."

"I'll do my best," Crystal said as she headed upstairs behind Kendu.

Upstairs Kendu just turned on some soft music and lay across the bed in deep thought. He so badly wanted to kill Perry. Not just because he had been calling the house, but more importantly, because he had stolen Diamond away from him. Just the thought of someone else having sex with Diamond had him ready to kill.

Crystal entered the room and sat on the bed next to him. "You all right?" she asked.

Kendu sighed. "Yeah, I'm fine."

"He'll stop calling." She slid on top of Kendu's back and began massaging him. "Don't even worry about that nonsense."

Kendu hated when people who wasn't built like that pretended to be. That's what bothered him the most. He so badly wanted to go over to Perry's house and beat the shit out of him, but Crystal and Diamond had talked him out of it.

"I just don't like that mufucka," Kendu said as he got up and stripped out of his clothes.

"Don't even waste your energy thinking about that psychopath." Crystal chuckled.

"You right, baby," Kendu then disappeared in the bathroom, so he could take a much-needed shower.

Chapter 21

Kendu pulled up in front of the spot. Today things just seemed a little different. There wasn't a bunch of soldiers standing around outside, and the place seemed a little more quiet than usual. He took one last hit from his blunt before tossing it in the grass as he headed inside. He walked inside Dirty Black's office and was shocked to see Amazon in a wheelchair.

"Damn! You all right?" Kendu asked.

Amazon smirked. "I'm fine. They must be crazy if they think this chair is going to stop me."

Kendu laughed, to try to hide the sadness in his face. "Where's Dirty Black?"

"You ain't hear?" Amazon said, looking up at Kendu.

"Hear what?"

"He got locked up last night. Him and Action Jackson had a shootout in the middle of the street."

"Get the fuck outta here! They gave him bail?"

"Not yet," Amazon said, shaking his head. "They got all kinds of charges they trying to stick to him. Come to find out, we all been under surveillance for the past year, according to his lawyer. So, as of today, we are officially retired."

"You can't be serious," Kendu said, not believing what he was hearing. All this time he thought Dirty Black was untouchable. Now, hearing that he was locked up came as a shock to him.

"Yup." Amazon smiled. "As of today you are a free man." He extended his hand.

Kendu quickly shook it. "It was a pleasure working with you."

"The pleasure was all mine," Amazon said, handing him a black plastic bag full of money. "My advice to you is, leave town sooner than later, and make sure you don't spend all that in one place."

Before Kendu could reply, he heard his cell phone ringing. "Hello," he answered.

"Hey, baby. Are you busy?" Crystal asked.

"No, baby. Why? What's up?"

"My car has been making a funny noise. Can you take it to the mechanic and get it looked at for me please?"

"No problem, baby. I'm on my way."

"I'm outta here." Amazon gave Kendu dap. "I'll see you at the top," he said, rolling out of Kendu's sight.

"Damn!" Kendu said out loud as he took in all the info he had just received. He couldn't believe how everything just came crumbling down so fast.

Kendu hopped in his car and headed home. After driving for about fifteen minutes, he decided to take heed to what Amazon had just told him and leave town. As he slowed down for the yellow light, he noticed a white man in a black Taurus that seemed to be following him. "Who the fuck is this?" he thought out loud as he tried to ditch the white guy, taking a few back streets.

After ten minutes of playing hide-and-seek, he thought he'd finally succeeded in ditching the white man when he no longer saw the Taurus in his rearview mirror.

"Yeah, it's definitely time to leave," he thought out loud as he pulled up in his driveway. He stepped inside his house and saw Diamond sitting on the couch looking sexy. "Hey."

"Hey. What's up?" Kendu said as the two slapped five. "Where's Crystal?"

"Her and Jessica went to the supermarket," Diamond told him. "I let her use my car 'cause she said something was wrong with hers."

"Yeah, I'm suppose to take it to the mechanic, so he can take a look at it. But first I need to talk to you about something."

Kendu poured two drinks and handed one to Diamond.

"What's on your mind?" Diamond asked as the two stood in the kitchen.

"Shit is starting to get hot. I think it's best if me and Crystal leave town."

"When?"

"Tonight."

"So I guess this means I'm never going to see you again, huh?"

"I mean, we will always be friends." Deep down Kendu did still love Diamond, but she had made the decision to leave, not him.

"I love you," Diamond said, moving in closer to him.

"I love you too."

Their lips connected.

"This ain't right," Kendu weakly protested as he tried to push Diamond away.

"I'm your wife," she said. "And I'm about to remind you just why you married me." Diamond pushed Kendu's back up against the refrigerator then slowly slid down to her knees.

Kendu was getting ready to protest again, but when he felt her soft lips on his penis, his words quickly got lost in his throat. "Damn!" he moaned, guiding her head with his hand.

Diamond grabbed Kendu's ass and forced him deeper into her mouth. She missed how he used to fill her mouth up.

Kendu pushed Diamond's head away and lifted her up, carrying her over to the counter, knocking down whatever was sitting on top as he laid her down gently. He lifted Diamond's sun dress, pushed her thong to the side, and kissed on her magic button.

"You missed your pussy, daddy?"

"Yes," Kendu said in a whisper. He slowly licked and sucked all over Diamond's clit. He buried his face in between her legs, working his tongue like a rattlesnake, forcing her to come for him.

"I need to feel my dick." Diamond slid off the counter and turned around. She placed her hands on the counter, arching her back and cocking her ass up in the air, so Kendu could enter her from behind.

"Ahhh!" she moaned as soon as she felt Kendu enter her walls. With each stroke Diamond made sure she threw her ass back, matching Kendu stroke for stroke.

Kendu grabbed a handful of Diamond's hair as he thrust in and out of her love tunnel, until finally exploding inside of her. He quickly pulled up his pants and walked over to the couch and flopped down.

"We shouldn't've done that." Kendu was mad at himself for what they'd just done. He thought he was stronger than that.

"Why not, baby?" Diamond asked, taking the seat next to him.

"Because I'm with someone. And that's not right. You didn't like it when it was being done to you, right?"

"Fuck that bitch!" Diamond spat. "It's always been us against the world." She wanted her husband back and didn't care what she had to do to make it happen. "I have the right to still fuck you. You are still my husband, remember?"

"It's not just that simple." Kendu got up and left Diamond sitting in the house alone.

He hopped in Crystal's car and headed towards the mechanic shop. He couldn't believe what he'd just done. He had tried his hardest to resist Diamond's touch, but for some reason, he just couldn't.

The way Diamond was talking before he'd left, he wasn't sure that she wouldn't tell Crystal what they'd just done. "Fuck!" He was mad at himself for being so weak. Now for the rest of the day that incident was going to be on his mind.

"Fuck!" Big Time cursed as he pulled up into the small mechanic shop. He had caught a flat tire on his way to meet up with Action Jackson. "Ayo', papi," he called out to the Spanish mechanic. "I need you take care of this flat for me and make it snappy." Big Time handed the man a hundred-dollar bill. As he waited he pulled out his cell phone and called up one of his honeys.

Kendu pulled into the empty spot in the small mechanic shop. He threw the car in park and had to do a quick double-take. He knew that wasn't who he thought it was.

After taking a better look, he couldn't believe his eyes. There Big Time stood all alone with his back turned to him on the phone. He reached for his waistline, but then he remembered leaving his gun on the counter while him and Diamond was getting busy, having sex. "Shit!"

Kendu reached in his pocket and removed his knife, and smoothly hopped out the car. He ran up on Big Time from behind and quickly plunged his knife in and out of his back repeatedly, until the man crumbled to the ground.

Just as Kendu was about to stab Big Time in the neck, he felt some cold steel being pressed to the back of his head.

"Put the knife down now!" the voice behind him ordered.

Kendu quickly did as he was told. Once the knife was out of his hand, the man behind him roughly tossed him to ground and handcuffed him. When Kendu looked up, he saw the same white guy who had been following him earlier in the day. Come to find out, the man following him was a cop. The white guy tossed Kendu in the back of his car and slammed the door.

"Fuck!" Kendu sat in the back of the cop car feeling stupid, but good at the same time. He had finally got his revenge on Big Time.

Seconds later he watched as an ambulance came and picked up Big Time and rushed him to the hospital.

Crystal made it back home and saw Diamond sitting on the couch. "Kendu didn't get back yet?" she asked, as her and Jessica struggled bringing all the groceries inside.

"Nah, not yet," Diamond answered, grabbing a couple of bags.

Crystal looked at the clock on the wall. It was 9:16 P.M. After going to the supermarket, she'd decided to take Jessica to see a movie, and she just knew that by the time she got back Kendu would have been home. "How long has he been gone for?"

"A few hours." Diamond went back to watching TV. "He should've been back by now though."

Crystal pulled out her cell phone and dialed his number, only to get the answering machine. "Something ain't right," she said out loud.

***

While Kendu sat in the holding cell waiting to get processed, he saw Action Jackson sitting in the cell across from him, and Amazon in the cell next to Action Jackson.

"I'ma kill you, muthafucka!" Action Jackson yelled from his cell, leaning up against the bars.

"You better go ask ya man Big Time what happened to him." Kendu laughed loudly.

"You caught that nigga?" Amazon yelled out from his cell.

"You know I did! I made him pay for what he did to you."

"My nigga." Amazon smiled. That was the best news he'd received all day.

"When I catch you, I'ma put you in a wheelchair, just like I did your friend!" Action Jackson yelled.

"Shut the fuck up!" a heavy-set C.O. yelled as he unlocked Kendu's cell and handcuffed him. "Y'all animals, save that bullshit for when y'all get to Rikers Island."

Action Jackson yelled at the C.O., "Fuck you too, you fat muthafucka!"

The C.O. smiled as he chained Kendu and placed him on the bus headed to Rikers Island. He then cuffed Action Jackson and placed him on the same bus on purpose.

"You a dead man!" Action Jackson yelled from the back of the bus. "I'm popping off as soon as they let us off the bus!"

Kendu ignored Action Jackson's threats, closing his eyes and trying to get some rest during the ride. He would deal with the man when they got off the bus.

***

Two days had passed, and Crystal still hadn't heard from Kendu. Ever since she and Kendu got together, he had never just disappeared for this long without calling. For the last forty-eight hours she had been up and awake, waiting for him to walk through the front door.

"If I don't hear from him in the next ten minutes, I'm going to start calling up the hospitals." She looked over at Diamond, who also looked worried.

Before Crystal could say another word, the house phone rang. "I know that's him," she said as she ran to the phone. "Hello?" she answered excitedly.

The only thing that could be heard was a man breathing on the other line.

Crystal immediately hung the phone up.

When the phone rang again, Crystal picked it up. "Listen, muthafucka, stop calling my house. You coward!"

"Baby, it's me," Kendu said.

"Baby?" Crystal yelled. "Is that you?"

"Yeah, it's me," Kendu replied.

"Where the fuck have you been? You had me scared to death," she said, worry in her voice.

"In jail. It's a long story, but I just came back from court, and these crackers tryin'-a pin all kind of shit on me."

"Did they give you bail?"

"Yeah. Seventy thousand. I need you to bring that money down here and get me out of here right now," he told her, not wanting to spend another second in the nasty jail.

"I'm on my way, daddy."

Crystal quickly ran upstairs to Kendu's safe, punched in the combination, and took out $90,000 just in case. She quickly tossed the money in her Louis Vuitton bag and headed back downstairs. "Can you keep an eye on Jessica for me until I get back?"

"Of course, I will." Diamond watched Crystal hurry out the door. Inside she felt bad that another woman was loving her husband the way she was supposed to love him. She had made a big mistake by leaving Kendu, and now she was paying for it.

Perry sat outside of Kendu's house staked out like he'd been doing every night. He wanted to kill Diamond so bad, his hand began to shake uncontrollably. He'd never wanted to kill a person more than he wanted to kill Diamond right now.

As he sat parked across the street he saw Crystal storm out of the house and hop in Diamond's car and zoom out of the driveway. Perry didn't know what was going on, but he knew he was tired of waiting. It was time for him to make a move. He hopped out of his car and walked over and popped the trunk. The first thing he did was remove his blue mechanic suit and put it on over his clothes. Once Perry zipped up his suit, he immediately felt invincible. He grabbed his duffel bag from out the trunk, headed towards the front door, and knocked lightly.

When Diamond heard someone knock on the door, she immediately thought it was Crystal. "She must've forgot something." She hopped up and ran to the door. She opened the door, and almost shit on herself when she saw who was on the other side.

Perry pushed his way inside the house before Diamond got a chance to close the door. "You thought you was going to get away from me, didn't you?" Perry growled as he slapped Diamond down to the floor. "Think you just going to steal my money then just run off into the sunset with the next nigga? I don't think so."

Diamond tried to crawl to the kitchen, but a sharp kick to her stomach stopped her dead in her tracks.

"Fuck you think you going?"

"Please, Perry, you don't have to do this," she begged.

Perry ignored her plea as he roughly sat her in a chair and duct-taped her hands and feet so she couldn't move.

Upstairs Jessica sat in her room watching TV, but when she heard a loud commotion downstairs, she quickly ran to the top of the stairs to see what was going on. From the top of the stairs she watched as a man in a blue jumpsuit roughly slammed Diamond onto a chair and began to quickly tape up her hands and feet so she couldn't move.

"Please, baby, don't do this," Diamond begged.

Perry looked at her and smacked the shit out of her. "Don't you ever fix your mouth to call me that!" He couldn't believe she had just tried to call him that, the nerve of her.

Diamond felt her nose bleeding as she watched Perry dig inside his duffel bag.

"I got something for you," he said with a devilish smile on his face as he removed an old-school slave whip from out of his bag and let it hang down to the floor.

"Please don't," Diamond cried.

Perry ripped her clothes off her body until she was completely naked. He smiled as he swung the whip and watched the tip of it land across her chest and tear open her soft skin. Just the sight of Diamond in pain brought a smile to Perry's face as he swung the whip repeatedly, whipping her like she was a slave.

The pain was so overbearing during the whipping, Diamond passed out twice, only to wake up to the same nightmare.

"Perry, please," she begged in a light whisper. Right about now she was willing to do anything to stop him from hitting her again. At that very moment, she regretted leaving Kendu. If she could go back in time right now, she definitely would have.

"Okay, I'm all done." Perry tossed the whip to the side. "Now it's time to clean you up." He reached in his bag and removed two bottles of rubbing alcohol and began splashing it all over her naked scarred-up body.

"Ahhhhhh!!!" Diamond screamed at the top of her lungs when she felt the rubbing alcohol sink into her open wounds.

"What you crying for?" Perry asked, still smiling from ear to ear. "We just now getting started." He reached down into his bag and removed a pair of clippers, which looked like a super-sized pair of scissors. "I got something real special for you."

Before Perry went back to work, he pulled out his penis and proceeded to urinate all over Diamond's face and the rest of her body. "You like that, don't you? You nasty bitch!" Perry placed Diamond's pinky finger in between the hedge clippers and snapped it off.

"You not only stole from me, but you was cheating on me with this Kendu clown the whole time, wasn't you?" Perry asked with a smirk on his face. "Wasn't you?" He smacked the shit out of Diamond.

"I never cheated on you, Perry." Blood dripped from Diamond's hand, where her pinky used to be. "I thought you didn't love me anymore, 'cause of how you just started hitting and beating on me out the blue. We can still work this out," she said, hoping her words would save her life. "Perry, baby, please give me another chance."

"Save it," Perry hushed her. "You ain't nothing but an ungrateful bitch, just like the rest of them." He placed

Diamond's ring finger in between the hedge clippers and snapped it off.

Diamond bit down on her bottom lip as she howled like a wounded animal. She was all out of ideas, and didn't know what else to do. She had never experienced this much pain in her life.

"I'm about to teach you what happens when you fuck with Perry." He smiled as he went on to the next finger.

Chapter 22

"Fuck!" Kendu cursed as he stepped out the jail with a frown on his face. He power-walked over to the all-white Audi that waited for him curbside.

Before he could reach the car, Crystal hopped out and slid in his arms. "Oh my God! Baby, I missed you so much!" she said, trying to squeeze the life out of him. "I thought something bad had happened to you." Crystal was overjoyed to see her man in one piece.

Kendu hopped in the passenger seat of the Audi. "We have to leave town tonight!" He knew there was no way the DA was going to let him or anybody from Dirty Black's crew get off easy.

"What they trying to hit you with?" Crystal asked as she pulled off.

"Everything," Kendu said, shaking his head. "These muthafuckas trying to hit me with shit I ain't never even heard of before."

"So what's the plan?"

"Soon as we get to the house, grab Jessica, a few things, and all the money we got up in the house and come right back out," Kendu said in a firm voice.

"What about Diamond?" Crystal didn't just want to leave her for dead like that, especially with Perry threatening her and all.

"I don't know what she's going to do. All I know is, we have to go." Kendu didn't have time to come up with a plan for Diamond. She would have to figure out what she was going to do on her own. He had his own problems to worry about.

Crystal pulled up in the driveway and kept the car running.

"Just grab a few things, and that's it," Kendu told her. "And hurry up!" he yelled. He watched Crystal go inside the house, while he waited in the passenger seat.

Soon as Crystal stepped inside the house she dropped her keys. When she picked them up and looked up, she froze in place.

Perry grabbed a handful of her hair as he roughly tossed her down on the floor. "So glad you could join us."

Before he could grab her again, Crystal had scrambled to her feet and ran to the kitchen and grabbed a sharp knife from off the rack. "You better back the fuck up!" She swung the knife back and forth in the air. "Take another step, and I'ma slice you the fuck up!" she said, trying to buy herself some time to think of her next move.

Crystal looked out the corner of her eye and saw how messed up Diamond's dead body looked, no fingers or toes, and her face all cut up. "Oh hell no," she said out loud. No way she was going to allow Perry to torture her like he'd just done to Diamond.

Perry tried to grab Crystal, but she quickly sliced his hand with the knife. He snatched his hand back. He reached down and picked up his whip from off the floor. "You wanna play games with me, bitch?" He swung the whip at Crystal's wrist, causing her to drop the knife.

"Shit!" Crystal grabbed her wrist that had a long whelp on it and was now bleeding.

"Get over here, bitch!" He knocked Crystal out with a punch to her temple. He watched as her head bounced off the floor like a basketball. He dragged her from the kitchen back to the living room by her ankle. Then he grabbed another chair from the kitchen and tossed her body in it. Then he taped her hands and feet together, so she couldn't move.

"All you women are all the same!" he huffed. He roughly snatched Crystal's clothes off until she was butt naked.

Crystal's eyes shot open when she felt the tip of the whip swipe across her chest.

"I'ma teach you some manners too." Perry forcefully swung the whip, whipping her like a runaway slave the same way he'd done Diamond.

Outside in the car, Kendu sucked his teeth. He looked at his watch and beeped the horn, signaling for Crystal to hurry up. "Fuck taking her so long?" he said to himself. "I told her to just grab a few things." Kendu hopped out the Audi and stretched his legs. He figured Crystal was inside giving Diamond the rundown on what was going on. He shook his head as he walked towards the door.

When he stepped inside, he was about say something, until he saw Perry with a whip in his hand in a swinging motion.

"Fuck is you doing?" Kendu yelled as he ran and tackled Perry.

The two men went crashing through the kitchen table and on to the floor. Kendu jumped on top of Perry and began raining blows on his face.

Perry lifted up and threw Kendu off him, and both men quickly hopped up on their feet. Perry reached down for his whip, but Kendu stepped on it and kneed Perry in his face.

"That's right. Kick his ass, baby!" Crystal said, cheering her man on from the sideline. "Kill that mufucka!"

Perry fell on the floor, on top of his duffel bag, and came up with a hammer in his hand, which he swung at Kendu's head.

Kendu partially blocked it, but the impact from the hammer dropped him.

Perry smiled as he gripped the hammer with two hands and raised it behind his back. Kendu, on the floor, closed his eyes to brace himself for the blow when he saw Perry coming down with the hammer. But before Perry could swing the hammer, Jessica jumped on his back and tried to choke him.

Perry quickly reached back with his hand, grabbed the back of Jessica's head as he bent over, and flung her to the floor like she was a rag doll, knocking the wind out of her.

"I see I'm going to have to teach this little bitch a lesson too," Perry said with a twisted smile on his face. He dug inside his duffel bag and pulled out a mini-sword. He raised it in the air. Just as he was about to come down with it, he felt four shots rip through his chest, dropping him immediately.

Kendu lay on the floor holding the .380 he had left on the counter for emergencies.

"Baby, are you all right?" Crystal yelled from the chair.

"Yes, baby, we are both fine." Kendu went inside his closet and pulled out his shotgun with the pistol grip and cocked one into the chamber as he walked over to Perry's body and stood over him.

"No, baby. Untie me first," Crystal said from the chair. "I want to shoot him in his face myself."

Kendu smiled at his woman. He looked over at Diamond's dead body and forced the tears not to come down. Deep down he still had love for Diamond and even though they couldn't be together, this was the last thing he wanted to see happen to her. He had to force himself not to look at her.

He reached down and picked up the mini-sword and walked over to Crystal. He sat the shotgun down by her feet as he began cutting the tape off her feet. Then he worked his way up to her wrist. Kendu cut the tape off one of her wrists. Just as he was about to cut the tape off her other wrist, he heard Crystal yell, "Watch out!"

Before Kendu even got a chance to turn around, Perry swung the hammer down with all his might, hitting him right on the top of his head and killing him instantly. He then climbed on top of Kendu and began beating his face in with the hammer until his face looked like red apple sauce.

"I'ma teach y'all muthafuckas about playing with me!" Perry growled as he walked back over to his duffel bag and removed an electric saw. He quickly found an outlet and plugged it in. "I'ma show you what happens when you fuck with Perry," he said, spit flying from his mouth with every word he spoke.

Perry suddenly dropped down to his knees as he looked directly at Crystal, and he began sawing off Jessica's arm. He smiled as he felt the saw cutting through her bone, the blood splashing up in his face and all over the place. He ignored Jessica's screams as he continued to saw away with a crazy look on his face.

Crystal screamed at the top of her lungs, "No! Please, that's my babbbbbyyyy!" she cried as she struggled to get her arm free. "Take me instead!"

"Don't worry, bitch. You're next!" Perry smiled as he pressed the saw down on Jessica's leg. "Here, hold this for me." He laughed as he tossed Jessica's leg at Crystal. Perry stayed on his knees until he chopped Jessica into little pieces. His face was covered with Jessica's blood, as he tossed the pieces of her body in a black garbage bag.

Once Perry was done, he stood up and turned towards Crystal. He immediately stopped dead in his tracks when he saw her standing there holding the shotgun with two hands.

"It was an accident," Perry said with a smile on his face. "I didn't mean to chop your daughter up like that. Now give me that gun before you do something stupid."

"Accident, *my ass*!" Crystal snarled as she pulled the trigger.

Boooooooom!

Crystal watched as his body hit the floor, and slid until it hit the wall. The shot was so loud that both of her ear drums were ringing.

"Muthafucka!" Crystal turned and grabbed the house phone. She dialed 9-1-1 and waited for someone to answer.

As she talked to the operator, Perry was slowly crawling back up to his feet behind her.

"Listen, bitch, just send help now!" Crystal yelled as she slammed down the phone in the operator's face.

When she turned around, Perry was gone. "What the fuck!" she said out loud as she looked around and didn't see him. Her head quickly turned towards the stairs when she heard footsteps running up the stairs.

"Fuck!" Crystal slowly inched her way up the steps one by one. When she reached the top of the steps, everything looked normal, but she knew he was up there somewhere, and there was no way she could let him leave the house alive. He had to die for what he did to Jessica.

She inched her way down the hallway, taking baby steps, until she reached the first room, which was the bathroom. Crystal slowly eased open the door with her foot as she stepped inside and turned the light on. The bathroom wasn't too big, but what scared her was, the shower curtain was pulled closed, so she couldn't tell if he was hiding in the bathtub or not.

She slowly eased her way over to the tub and took a deep breath. Once she got close enough, she quickly snatched the shower curtain back as she let out a frightened nervous scream. She quickly caught her breath when she saw the bathtub was empty.

Crystal swiftly exited the bathroom and made her way towards the next room, which was the master bedroom. She stepped inside the room and turned the light on. She slowly eased her way over to Kendu's closet first. She snatched open the door and was thankful when she saw nothing in there except for Kendu's belongings.

"Fuck!" Crystal cursed, looking at her king-sized bed. She knew that in order to check under there she would have to put the shotgun down. "Shit!" She sat the shotgun on the floor and quickly checked under the bed. She exhaled when she didn't find nothing under there.

Crystal stood up to her feet, and just as she re-gripped the shotgun, out of the corner of her eye, she saw Perry running full speed at her. She aimed the shotgun at his chest, closed her eyes, and pulled the trigger.

Booooom!

The shot hit Perry in his chest, but it didn't slow him down as he tackled Crystal like a linebacker, and the two went crashing out the window. The fall from the window felt like it was a slow-motion dream to Crystal, until her body hit the ground like a sack of potatoes.

Five minutes later, she woke up with police and paramedics all around her.

An officer shined his flashlight in her face. "Ma'am, are you all right?"

Crystal quickly hopped up off the ground. "Where is he? Where is he?" she screamed, looking around, a frantic look on her face. She knew Perry was still close by. Even though the police were there, she still didn't feel safe.

"Where is who?" the officer asked.

"He's going to kill me!" Crystal screamed.

"Ma'am, calm down," the officer yelled as they all carried Crystal into the back of the ambulance and strapped her down.

"He killed everybody!" Crystal screamed, struggling to get free.

Detective Washington walked out of the house with a disgusted look on his face. He made his way over to the back of the ambulance. "Everybody out!" he yelled. "I need to talk to her alone." He watched everyone exit the ambulance. He was now in charge of the case and planned on running it his way.

"He killed everybody!" Crystal said frantically.

"I know he did," Detective Washington told her. "We've been trying to track this killer down for years now. Did you happen to see his face?"

"Yes, I saw his face. I know his name, I know where he works at and everything." Crystal broke down crying. "He killed my daughter," she said, tears just streaming down her face nonstop. All she could think of was the sick images of her daughter being sawed into little pieces.

"Dont worry. I've just been assigned to this case, and I promise you, I'm going to catch this psycho," Detective Washington said. "Let's get you downtown and away from all this madness, so we can hurry up and catch this fucka." He covered Crystal's naked body with a sheet then decided to ride the ambulance with her.

Detective Washington had been trying to track Perry down for the past two years, and now with Crystal's help, he had a better chance at catching the pyscho. He was just happy that Crystal was alive. Finally he had an eyewitness.

"I shot him twice," Crystal said in between sobs as the ambulance pulled off.

Perry pulled up in his driveway and quickly hopped out his car. He jogged to his front door and hurried inside. He tossed all his money inside a duffel bag, grabbed two suits from his closet, and was right back out the door. He knew he had to get out of town, and do it fast. He couldn't believe what had just happened. Not only did Crystal almost kill him, but he also had to hurry up and flee the scene before the cops arrived. He thought about killing Crystal before he left, but he didn't have enough time.

Perry removed the metal chest protector that he wore over his Kevlar vest from under his shirt and tossed it on the ground. The vest had saved him from being killed, but he was in tremendous pain. The shots he took broke a few of his ribs, but he didn't have time to feel pain. He had to get up out of town.

Perry hopped in his BMW and hit the highway, not knowing where he was headed. All he knew was, he had to get as far away from New York as possible. As he drove, the only thing on his mind was Crystal. He looked at himself through the rearview mirror and smiled. There was no way he planned on letting her get away like that. She would definitely be seeing him again. And sooner than she imagined.

To Be Continued

Notes

Notes

Notes

ORDER FORM
URBAN BOOKS, LLC
78 E. Industry Ct
Deer Park, NY 11729

Name: (please print):_____

Address: _____

City/State: _____

Zip: _____

QTY	TITLES	PRICE

Shipping and handling-add $3.50 for 1st book, then $1.75 for each additional book.
Please send a check payable to:
Urban Books, LLC
Please allow 4-6 weeks for delivery

ORDER FORM
URBAN BOOKS, LLC
78 E. Industry Ct
Deer Park, NY 11729

Name:(please print):_____

Address: _____

City/State: _____

Zip: _____

QTY	TITLES	PRICE
	16 On The Block	$14.95
	A Girl From Flint	$14.95
	A Pimp's Life	$14.95
	Baltimore Chronicles	$14.95
	Baltimore Chronicles 2	$14.95
	Betrayal	$14.95
	Black Diamond	$14.95
	Black Diamond 2	$14.95
	Black Friday	$14.95
	Both Sides Of The Fence	$14.95
	Both Sides Of The Fence 2	$14.95
	California Connection	$14.95

Shipping and handling-add $3.50 for 1st book, then $1.75 for each additional book.
Please send a check payable to:
Urban Books, LLC
Please allow 4-6 weeks for delivery

ORDER FORM
URBAN BOOKS, LLC
78 E. Industry Ct
Deer Park, NY 11729

Name: (please print): _____

Address: _____

City/State: _____

Zip: _____

QTY	TITLES	PRICE
	California Connection 2	$14.95
	Cheesecake And Teardrops	$14.95
	Congratulations	$14.95
	Crazy In Love	$14.95
	Cyber Case	$14.95
	Denim Diaries	$14.95
	Diary Of A Mad First Lady	$14.95
	Diary Of A Stalker	$14.95
	Diary Of A Street Diva	$14.95
	Diary Of A Young Girl	$14.95
	Dirty Money	$14.95
	Dirty To The Grave	$14.95

Shipping and handling-add $3.50 for 1st book, then $1.75 for each additional book.

Please send a check payable to:
Urban Books, LLC
Please allow 4-6 weeks for delivery

ORDER FORM
URBAN BOOKS, LLC
78 E. Industry Ct
Deer Park, NY 11729

Name:(please print):_____

Address: _____

City/State: _____

Zip: _____

QTY	TITLES	PRICE
	Gunz And Roses	$14.95
	Happily Ever Now	$14.95
	Hell Has No Fury	$14.95
	Hush	$14.95
	If It Isn't love	$14.95
	Kiss Kiss Bang Bang	$14.95
	Last Breath	$14.95
	Little Black Girl Lost	$14.95
	Little Black Girl Lost 2	$14.95
	Little Black Girl Lost 3	$14.95
	Little Black Girl Lost 4	$14.95
	Little Black Girl Lost 5	$14.95

Shipping and handling-add $3.50 for 1st book, then $1.75 for each additional book.
Please send a check payable to:
   Urban Books, LLC
Please allow 4-6 weeks for delivery

ORDER FORM
URBAN BOOKS, LLC
78 E. Industry Ct
Deer Park, NY 11729

Name: (please print):_____

Address: _____

City/State: _____

Zip: _____

QTY	TITLES	PRICE
	Loving Dasia	$14.95
	Material Girl	$14.95
	Moth To A Flame	$14.95
	Mr. High Maintenance	$14.95
	My Little Secret	$14.95
	Naughty	$14.95
	Naughty 2	$14.95
	Naughty 3	$14.95
	Queen Bee	$14.95
	Say It Ain't So	$14.95
	Snapped	$14.95
	Snow White	$14.95

Shipping and handling-add $3.50 for 1st book, then $1.75 for each additional book.
Please send a check payable to:
Urban Books, LLC
Please allow 4-6 weeks for delivery

ORDER FORM
URBAN BOOKS, LLC
78 E. Industry Ct
Deer Park, NY 11729

Name:(please print):_____

Address: _____

City/State: _____

Zip: _____

QTY	TITLES	PRICE
	Spoil Rotten	$14.95
	Supreme Clientele	$14.95
	The Cartel	$14.95
	The Cartel 2	$14.95
	The Cartel 3	$14.95
	The Dopefiend	$14.95
	The Dopeman Wife	$14.95
	The Prada Plan	$14.95
	The Prada Plan 2	$14.95
	Where There Is Smoke	$14.95
	Where There Is Smoke 2	$14.95

Shipping and handling-add $3.50 for 1st book, then $1.75 for each additional book.

Please send a check payable to:

Urban Books, LLC

Please allow 4-6 weeks for delivery